A Wooden Ship
and
A Tin Can

A Wooden Ship and a Tin Can

On the wall to the left was a photo of Captain Cassin Young. Gordon stopped and studied the picture of the man after whom the destroyer was named.

What was it like to have a ship named in your memory, he asked himself. It was probably the same for the people who had cities, buildings, and playing fields named after them.

Gordon tapped the tips of his fingers of his left hand on the picture. He swooned and blacked out for a moment.

When he regained his senses and his balance, Gordon was sitting on the deck of a ship, not the *Cassin Young*.

Where am I? It's not Charlestown? What kind of ship is this? It's kind of ugly. Holy crap, is that the U.S.S. Arizona *next to it?*

The cold and gray of the Boston Navy Yard was replaced by a soft, warm wind and bright, early morning sunshine. Then he noticed he sat in a harbor with many ships, U.S. Navy ships. There were palm trees. This wasn't Charlestown, Massachusetts.

Gordon grew nervous. He had a very bad feeling about where he was.

A Wooden Ship
and
A Tin Can

Mike Ryan

A Wings ePress, Inc.
Young Adult Novel

Wings ePress, Inc.

Edited by: Jeanne Smith
Copy Edited by: Christie Kraemer
Executive Editor: Jeanne Smith
Cover Artist: Trisha FitzGerald-Jung
Ship: Pixabay, Planes Pexel

All rights reserved

Names, characters and incidents depicted in this book are products of the author's imagination or are used fictitiously. Any resemblance to actual events, locales, organizations, or persons, living or dead, is entirely coincidental and beyond the intent of the author or the publisher.

No part of this book may be reproduced or transmitted in any form or by any means, electronic or mechanical, including photocopying, recording, or by any information storage and retrieval system, without permission in writing from the publisher.

Wings ePress Books
www.wingsepress.com

Copyright © 2024 by: Mike Ryan
ISBN 978-8-89197-998-7

Published In the United States Of America

Wings ePress, Inc.
3000 N. Rock Road
Newton, KS 67114

Dedication

This one's for Steve, my little brother.

Prologue

Not One for the Water

Ever since he was a young child, Marty Beckwith always wanted a boat. His stepfather, Doug McGregor, took him to Folkstone Pond in Tiot, a western Boston suburb. St. Patrick Catholic Church overlooked the pond, which might have qualified as a lake. There was a town boat landing adjacent to the church parking lot. In the good weather, some Catholics skipped Mass for a ride on the silvery water.

Marty's birth father, Gary, had been killed in Vietnam when he was a year old. His stepdad had also served in the same war, and Marty had never known his real dad.

Doug had roped a canoe atop an old Woodie station wagon. He parked the black 1963 Buick. Marty was five. He was already a good swimmer. His stepfather untied the rope and pulled the canoe carefully from the roof. Doug was a strong man with a Marine tattoo on each forearm. Once he got the canoe on the ground, he opened the back door to pull out a life preserver. Motioning to Marty, he tied the vest on his son.

"I'll paddle, Marty. You enjoy the ride." He smiled. "Please stay still. We don't want to tip over."

"Sure, Dad. Can I paddle?"

"Maybe in a few years."

Doug carried the canoe onto the concrete and lowered it into the water. He stepped into the pond, picked up Marty, and placed him in the front. The paddler slowly climbed in. He lit a Marlboro and started to row. Enshrouded in cigarette smoke, the craft skimmed across the calm water. Marty looked at folks stepping out of church after noon Mass. He waved to a few parishioners, and they waved back. Next, he looked at the water and saw small fish darting about.

Doug puffed and paddled. "What do you think, Marty?'

"Dad, this is cool. Can we go faster?

Doug chuckled. "We could, but just enjoy the ride."

Marty couldn't remember a better day. As he got older, there would be other canoe trips where he would eventually paddle while Doug sat and enjoyed his Marlboros. Folkstone Pond saw more motorized transport and water skiing on its waters. Marty noticed girls liked the faster water movement; some enjoyed the skiing.

He later asked his father," Can we get a boat with a motor?"

"Too expensive. Save your money. Besides, where would I put it during the off-season?"

"In the back yard," answered Marty.

"I really don't think your mother would go for it. I can fit the canoe in the garage, but not any kind of a bigger boat."

Even as a boy, Marty had envisioned a career playing in the National Hockey League. With that kind of money, he could afford a good-sized boat, maybe even a cabin cruiser.

Although the hockey dream had sunk after a college car accident, the boat dream survived.

~ * ~

Now, years later, as an adult and a father, Marty bought a little boat to fly over Folkstone Pond. The cabin cruiser would have to wait. He first wanted a craft for freshwater. Salt water would be his next quest.

Marty had bought the boat and trailer, and they rested in his driveway for a week. His wife, Martha, wasn't happy over that load on her property. She had grown up in coastal Maine and enjoyed sailing and boating. Martha would have preferred a boat docked in the ocean and not plopped on her property.

Their son Gordon learned to swim at the outdoor Folkstone Municipal Pool. As he grew older, Gordon would've preferred an in-ground pool in their back yard. A boat made no difference to him. Getting his license later in the year was more important.

Marty tried fishing with Gordon, but waiting impatiently for fish to conveniently attach themselves to his hook held no appeal for Gordon. When his father would dash off for deep-sea fishing with a few friends, Gordon politely turned down the offer to join the expedition. Gordon was a landlubber and proud of it. Marty was disappointed his son had caught no love of catching fish or of boating.

A few years later, Marty dragged him out for the initial boat ride on Folkstone Pond. Gordon had really wanted to play wiffleball with his friend, Moose Marini. But on Sunday mornings, Moose attended Mass at St. Patrick's and wasn't available until after lunch.

On a spring morning, the two Beckwiths had risen early, showered, eaten breakfast, and driven two miles to the pond. Marty backed up his Ford truck to ease the trailer into the water. After Marty parked the truck, the two of them climbed into the white boat, *Puck Beauty*. The captain started the engine and eased their way from the landing.

"Isn't this great, Gordo? Beautiful day for a ride. I could have brought the fishing equipment, but I just wanted to break her out for the first trip."

Gordon's stomach started to talk to him. His father had cooked a hearty breakfast of pancakes, scrambled eggs, and ham. Although the boat sailed smoothly and slowly, the discomfort intensified as his father increased the speed. Gordon's stomach started to churn.

They twirled around the pond. No other boats had joined them. Marty was so enjoying his driving, he didn't realize his son was curled up in a fetal position on the floor. Marty zipped around the lake's perimeter. He wondered what his stepdad would've thought of this cruiser. When they finally returned to the boat ramp, St. Pat's parishioners were breaking from church after the ten o'clock Mass. When the engine stopped, Gordon vomited over the side.

Marty felt bad. "Gordo, I didn't realize you were seasick."

Dizzy and light-headed, Gordon wiped his mouth. "I didn't either."

Gordon felt lousy for most of the day. When he saw Moose in school the next day, his friend said, "My dad said after Mass some kid was puking by the boat ramp. He said the kid looked like you."

"Moose, it was me. I never felt so crappy in my life. I never want to go out like that on the water again."

One

Gordon on the Rebound

Since the spring of his freshman year, Gordon Beckwith had started lifting weights. He needed to withstand fierce checks when opposing hockey players tried to outmuscle him in the corners or around the net. As a sophomore, he thought he had a great season. In March, Tiot High School advanced to the semi-finals before losing to Hingham High School four to zero. He thought that game was his worst of the year and felt he had let the team down. No one could talk to him for two weeks, not even his mother and father. His ex-girlfriend, Abbie Fortune, tried unsuccessfully. Finally, Marty Beckwith saw his son on his bed in his room staring at the ceiling.

"Gordo, you there?" he asked.

Gordon didn't move a muscle.

"Gordo, you in a coma?"

"No. I can't get over that game."

Marty sat down on the bed. "You know what? Losing sucks. Nobody likes it. But you have to move on. You did your best."

"I was horrible."

"I agree it wasn't your best game, but I think you let your temper get the best of you. You of all people got two penalties in that game."

Gordon shot up. "Which turned into two goals. I was getting a lot of cheap shots."

"Gordon, you've put up with that in the past. You let them bother you. Hingham knew they had to break your rhythm. They put a shadow on you the whole game."

"The guy was always on me. I got speared a couple of times, and the refs never called it."

"Hockey isn't golf. You've been beaten up and survived."

"I guess so." Gordon swung himself beside his father.

"You had a good year in soccer and in hockey. You made all hockey all-scholastic as a sophomore. That's a big deal, but don't make it a big deal. Stay humble."

"I'll try."

Marty ruffled his hair. "Enough self-pity. Get back to your weights. You're still growing in height and in muscle. Do you think Tom Brady ever gave up after his perfect season was ruined? He lost a few Super Bowls, but he kept working."

"You're right, Dad. I've been a dink. I haven't talked to Moose in ages."

Marty stood. "You haven't ignored your studies?"

Gordon grinned. "That I haven't. I'm trying to bring up my class rank. I want to be in the top five starting junior year."

"What's Abbie's rank?"

"Number two. I should find out mine soon."

"How's she doing?"

"She's in a couple of my classes."

"Do you talk?"

"We're cool."

"Good. She's a nice kid."

"She is."

Marty was about to leave. "Summer's coming up, and you're escaping—for the most part—working for me except for some weekends."

Marty owned two liquor stores, both in Foxboro. One was located on Route 1 near the stadium and his own parking lot; the new one was in Foxboro Center near the common. Gordon usually worked the Route 1 place along with the adjoining parking lot.

"I guess so."

"Looking forward to the new job?"

"I am. The Boston Navy Yard has so much history."

"*Old Ironsides* is one of the six frigates commissioned by President John Adams. Undefeated in battle, she's the oldest Navy ship."

"Plus, you have the World War Two destroyer, U.S.S. *Cassin Young*. I can't wait to check her out. You and Mom took me to the *Constitution*."

"I'd like to check the destroyer as well. Maybe Mom would too. Shipbuilding and the Navy are in her family."

"I learned a lot last fall when we went up to check out the University of Maine. It's a different way of life up there. It's too bad we don't see Mom's family."

"Gordon, you know I'm not much of a fan."

"That's too bad."

"Your grandmother thinks her daughter didn't marry well enough. She wasn't crazy about me, a broken-down hockey player."

"Mom's happy she's with us. Right?"

"You and I are both lucky to have her."

Gordon felt bad because he didn't know his grandmother and couldn't remember the last time he had seen her. Grandma McKinley never forgot his birthdays and Christmases. Gordon's mom usually took solo trips to visit her.

As he was about to close the door, Marty said, "Learn from losing. Keep working."

"I will. Thanks."

Losing still hurts.

Two

New Summer Directions

Gordon focused on his studies and found he had little time for any kind of mayhem. He shared classes with Abbie Fortune in biology and history. He missed her as a girlfriend, but they had agreed to go their separate ways for this year. They still talked and texted.

Gordon also missed Lizzie Soares from his job last summer, but there was too much distance between them. He lived in Tiot, and she lived forty miles away in Plymouth. There had been a few phone conversations and texts, but they faded as the pace of the school year quickened.

His priority wasn't romance, but academics and sports. In May of his sophomore year, Gordon had an appointment with his guidance counselor, Gladys Funk. He arranged a time to see her when he had a rare study hall.

Mrs. Funk looked like someone's grandmother with gray wavy hair pulled back in a bun, a rosy complexion, round-rimmed glasses, and a pearl necklace. She had worked at THS for four decades. Most students considered her aloof and sometimes stiff.

A secretary waved Gordon into the counselor's office.

"Good morning, Gordon," she said.

"Hi, Mrs. Funk. How are you today?"

"Better when I meet with a student who's on the rise."

Gordon wasn't sure how to respond. She motioned for him to sit.

"Class ranks have been set." Mrs. Funk tugged at her pearls. "I have the pleasure to tell you your rank is five, up five from last year. Congratulations, Gordon."

"Ah, um, that's great." Gordon cleared his throat.

"Are you looking at schools for after graduation?"

"I was thinking U-Maine in Orono."

"That's a fine school. We have several faculty members here who are alumni."

"My parents went there. They have a great hockey program."

She grinned. "I know of your hockey talents. Do you aspire to go pro?"

"Every kid who laces up his skates would love to do that. The chances are slim to get there."

"Your father was an outstanding player, although I believe he took a casual attitude to his studies."

"He buckled down in college, and he's done well in business."

"That's good to hear. What kind of vocation would you like to pursue if you're not playing for the Boston Bruins?"

Gordon smiled. "Teaching history and coaching hockey."

"Lord knows we need good teachers, especially nowadays with teachers facing so much pressure." She closed up his folder. "Have you thought about going beyond college? Perhaps go for a master's or a doctorate? What about a career in law or in medicine? Or become a professor of history?"

"I love history, Mrs. Funk, and I love hockey. There is something special about both of them. I'd like to stay connected to them."

"Gordon, I saw your junior high folder. You had some disciplinary problems in seventh grade. You got suspended. Then you had a turnaround in eighth grade and have kept up your grades since then. What's the story?"

"I wanted to take a break from hockey. My dad agreed only if my marks improved. I will admit I had a bad attitude back then, but hopefully, I've matured."

His counselor put out her hand, and Gordon shook it. "I appreciate your honesty. Your goal is a good one, but don't be afraid to look at other possibilities. The sky is the limit."

"Thank you."

"Come by and see me anytime."

Mrs. Funk thought to herself, *that boy could be anything he wanted to be. There was something different about this scholar-athlete. He's a lot different than his father.*

When school was dismissed at two-twenty-two, Gordon exited the building at the same time as Abbie Fortune.

"Hey, Abbie!"

"Hey, Gordon."

"Going my way?" he asked.

"Yes."

At the bottom of the steps, they veered to the left. "Abbie, did you get your class rank?"

"I did. Did you?"

"Yes. I have Mrs. Funk for guidance."

"I have Mr. Petrocelli. What's your number? You have to be in the top ten."

"Five," he replied. "What's yours?"

"Two."

"Two? That's fantastic. Who's number one?"

"I'm not sure, but I'd put my money on Lisa Galanis."

"She's very quiet and rarely answers in class."

"She's very nice, she's very pretty, and she likes you. Lisa always smiles when you answer in history class."

Gordon stopped walking. "Really?"

"Gordon, sometimes you're oblivious about things. The other day Lisa grabbed me after class and asked about us. I told her we were apart."

"What did she say?"

"Nothing. She just smiled and walked away."

Gordon had noticed Lisa's dark brown eyes, black hair, and bright smile.

Abbie nudged him. "You should ask her out."

"I'm too busy."

Gordon felt the urge to hug Abbie, but he kept walking.

Their route took them through Folkstone Cemetery. They stopped in front of Archie Folkstone's mausoleum. He had been a friend of theirs.

"Abbie, did your father get remarried?" Gordon asked."

"Yes, in the fall. And I'm going to have a half-sister or a half-brother at any moment."

"Did you go to the wedding?"

"Yes."

"Was it weird seeing your father take up a new wife?"

"Sort of, but my parents hadn't really been together since he returned from his five-year disappearance. He's very happy with his new wife. I like her."

"What's she like?"

"Younger than Dad. Her name is Theresa, and she works at the dealership with him. She's a little rough around the edges, but she's good for him."

"How's Mom?"

"She commutes to Boston, and she's got a boyfriend."

"Really?"

"Mark Preston, the secretary of state."

"My old boss. He's a good guy. Do you like him?"

"He treats her well. He's never been married."

"Lots of changes with the Fortune family."

Abbie smiled. "Yes, indeed."

At the entrance to the cemetery, they were about to split up.

Gordon asked, "What's up for the summer?"

"Mom's trying to get me a job at the state library. If so, we would commute together."

"I think you'd love it working in town."

"What about you? I know you're not going back to the State House."

"Abbie, I haven't told you everything about what happened there last summer."

"What about your hot girlfriend?" Abbie had caught a glimpse of Gordon's co-worker, Lizzie Soares, when she accompanied her mother to the State House. She had seen Gordon and Lizzie talking and had freaked out.

"Abbie, she wasn't my girlfriend. Yes, we spent some time together. It was nothing special like you and me."

Abbie blushed. "I'm sorry. I guess I'm still jealous. My mother saw the two of you outside the library and didn't tell me until later."

"I can't go back to that job."

"You didn't like it?"

"Oh, I loved the job, loved being in the building. I, I—"

Abbie waved her hand. "Don't tell me, Gordon. You have tunnel fatigue?"

"Yes." He told her this time with more details about the tunnel in the basement of the State House, how he had first met Benedict Arnold in the Maine wilderness and returned a second time to the tunnel to rescue a jealous co-worker who slipped back into the past.

"Gordon, you are touched by history. You had told me you found another tunnel, but you hadn't told me all this. You were with Arnold at Saratoga?"

"Remember Mr. Perkins in history class talking Arnold's leg statue in eighth grade? I was there when he was shot in that leg. My parents and I took trip to Saratoga last fall and saw the Arnold boot statue."

"Why his leg?"

"Because he later turned traitor, Arnold couldn't be commemorated with a bust or a conventional statue. His name isn't even mentioned in the statue's inscription."

"Wow. So instead, will you work for your father this summer?"

"I got a job at the *Constitution* Museum in Charlestown. There are two ships, the *U.S.S. Constitution*, "Old Ironsides," and the *U.S.S. Cassin Young*, a World War Two destroyer."

"There shouldn't be any tunnels on two ships."

"I hope not. Maybe, we'll run into each other taking the train in and out of Boston."

Abbie smiled. "I'd like that."

Three

Why Marty Avoids Bath

Martha Beckwith felt she needed to see more of her mother. They spoke weekly on the phone, but Martha felt guilty about not driving enough to Bath, Maine. She decided to visit, and Gordon agreed to go with her.

Before they left, Gordon and his father were in Marty's room with his diorama of the Battle of Saratoga.

Once again, Gordon asked, "Why don't you go to see Mom's family?"

"I've told you why, Gordo," replied Marty as he set up several blue Continental soldiers on the right flank. "Your grandmother never approved of me because I wasn't smart or as handsome as Martha's old boyfriend."

"Why's that?"

"Grandma Agnes had set her sights on Curtis Bakewell, who dated your mother at Morse High School, home of the

Shipbuilders. She always viewed me as a poor substitute for her baby girl. Your mother was a surprise baby, the youngest by ten years. The two boys left home and never returned, and the two girls didn't have much to do with their baby sister. You can't blame them. They weren't interested in babysitting, although they were pissed off the few times they had to watch her."

Marty surveyed the battlefield. He placed Benedict Arnold on his black charger on the left flank. Gordon approved of the placement.

Marty picked up his light blue U-Maine hockey mug and sipped his black coffee.

"There was another reason Mom's sisters disliked her."

"Why was that?"

"Your mother was, and still is, drop dead gorgeous."

"They were jealous of her?"

"Inga and Helga inherited their father's genes. They weren't unattractive, but they were taller and big boned. Martha was her mother's double. Even after having five kids, Agnes kept herself in great shape. She was athletic and loved to skate. I've seen pictures of your grandmother when she was younger, and you would think it was your mother."

"They hated their sister?"

"Hate is too strong. Jealous probably. Martha not only was good looking, but she was a standout athlete and scholar like her mother."

"Field hockey and softball."

"Correct. I was hockey all the way. Sure, I played other sports as a kid, but hockey was my passion. That was going to be my ticket out of Tiot. I was a lazy student."

"What was my grandfather like?"

"Your grandfather Buster was a good guy," said Marty, as he started to paint the legs of the miniature figure of General Horatio Gates. Out of all the many American and British figures, Marty, who detested Gates, painted him last. "Never said much. Agnes, your grandmother, ran the show. Buster was happy to stay in the background."

"He was a World War Two veteran."

"Yes, he dropped out of high school before graduation and signed up for the Navy a few months before Pearl Harbor. Saw a lot of action and came home five years later."

"I wish I had known him."

"You were a baby when he passed. You would've liked him."

Marty took his time painting. Gordon shivered looking at the battlefield. Little did his father know, Gordon had stepped on historic Saratoga a few months ago.

"Why does Grandma hate you?"

"Again, I wouldn't call it hate, maybe a deep disgust with her daughter's choice of a mate. She thinks her baby threw her life away on a washed-up hockey player who doesn't go to church."

"But you're a college graduate and a successful businessman."

"Agnes envisioned Martha as the First Lady of Bath, or of Maine, if she had married Curtis Bakewell."

"Mom picked you."

"Damn right. I'm blessed to have her as a wife; you're blessed to have her as a mother."

"How come we don't go to church?"

"Agnes thinks I made your mother an atheist. My stepdad was a believer, but he never forced religion on me. My mother showed up at church on Christmas and Easter. She kept her beliefs to herself. Your mother was born Catholic, and maybe I was a bad influence on her, so she stopped going. She still believes in God."

"I have no religion."

"You're free to choose. I know you've gone to Mass several times with Moose's family."

"I liked the priest who said the Mass. Moose said the priest had played hockey when he was younger."

"Go with your gut, Gordon. Agnes probably will try to convert you when you see her. She'll turn you into a God-fearing Catholic Democrat. Be strong: stand your ground."

Marty chuckled. "I'm kidding. Agnes is still your grandmother. It will be good for you to see her. She is getting up there in age. Please give her my regards."

Gordon wasn't sure what to make of all this. It was the first time any light had been shed on the maternal side of his family. He knew about McKinley relatives, but Gordon had never met them. Gordon was looking forward see his grandmother.

Four

Maine Roots

Martha Beckwith had two brothers, Harold and Lars, and two sisters, Inga and Helga. Those four older siblings had moved out of state. Martha had a cousin, Delia Cummings, with whom she was close growing up who still lived in Maine. The two of them spoke regularly on the telephone. Martha exchanged greeting cards with her sisters. There was little or no connection with her brothers.

Her mother, Agnes Swenson McKinley, still lived in the family home near the city center. Her father Ross "Buster" McKinley died of lung cancer fifteen years ago. Like many in his family, he was a shipbuilder.

After serving in the Navy, he worked as an electrician at the Bath Iron Works for many years. Although his career was spent in marine construction on the Kennebec River, Buster wasn't a fan of swimming or boating. "I did enough of it when I was a kid and when I was in the Navy," he often told his family. "I work on the water and live by it. I don't need to go on it."

He loved pitching horseshoes at the American Legion, smoking, sipping ale, and keeping tabs on the Boston Red Sox. Buster stood six feet tall two inches with two hundred twenty pounds of muscle. His wife was five-foot four and slender. Buster lived for her and his two sons and three daughters.

Inga and Helga worried when dates picked them up at the house. Dad opened the door and could be quite intimidating. Although Mr. McKinley was always polite, just his presence scared off a few suitors. By the time Martha started dating, Mom greeted the males while Buster sat in the den watching television. Martha's two sisters said she had it easy because Dad didn't subject her dates to interrogation like he had for theirs.

When folks asked Buster what he did for work, he always replied, "I build ships. I live in the 'City of Ships.'"

Granted, he had the assistance of a horde of other workers to complete the task at the Bath Iron Works.

Martha's son hadn't visited his grandmother in quite a long time. Grandma Agnes always asked about Gordon and followed his hockey career. She had loved to skate throughout her life and was a better skater than her husband. Arthritis had curtailed her skating in recent years.

Marty pleaded he was too busy for the trip. Martha smirked and knew he would use work as his excuse.

"Marty, it's just one night."

"Dear, it's the Memorial Day weekend. The second store just opened, and there's an NCAA lacrosse tournament at the stadium."

She turned to her son. "Would you come with me, Gordon? Grandma would love to see you."

"Sure. I like Maine. I haven't gone since Dad took me to U-Maine."

His parents smiled. Gordon had bailed out his father.

~ * ~

The next Saturday morning, mother and son drove up to Maine. Gordon had his learner's permit, so Martha allowed him to take over the wheel for the short slice of New Hampshire on Rt. 95, across the Piscatagua River, and finally pulling over at the rest stop in Kittery, Maine. Gordon was a little nervous driving on the highway, but he stayed in the right lane, and grew more comfortable after a few miles.

On the drive through northern Maine, Gordon stopped reading *Six Frigates* by Ian Toll.

"Dad gave me some background about his relationship with Grandma."

Gordon summarized his recent conversation with his father.

Martha laughed as they pulled off Route 95 and pulled into a Dunkin' Donuts in Newburyport.

She said, "That sounds right. Mom put all her hopes on me. The other four kids turned out okay, but they were their own selves. I was the closest to her in personality and interests."

"What was my grandfather like?"

Martha ordered large two hot teas to go. "He was the opposite of my mother. Quiet. Liked his Budweiser and his non-filtered Lucky Strikes."

"Did your parents get along?"

"For the most part, my mother called the shots, but if my father disagreed with her, he simply stared and said, 'Agnes.' That settled her down."

"I wish I had known him."

"I think serving in the Navy had a profound effect upon him. He was a teenager who dropped out of high school and spent five years in the Pacific. After the war, he got a job at the shipyard. Became an electrician and married my mother."

"Did he ever talk about the war?"

"Rarely. If he had more than a few beers, he might mumble something about Pearl Harbor. He would whisper, 'Martha, it was like a bad dream, but it wasn't.'"

After receiving their teas, they let them steep for a minute, took out the bags, and stirred sugar into them.

"Funny thing about my father. He refused to buy Japanese cars. Always bought American. I'd ask him why. He'd point out today's Japanese carmakers had built planes and other equipment during the war."

Back on the Maine Turnpike, Gordon said, "My uncles also were in the military?"

"Both served in the Air Force for twenty years and retired. Dad never encouraged them, but they signed up after their senior years in high school. Harold lives in Colorado Springs, working at the Air Force Academy. Lars lives in San Diego; he sells real estate."

"Do they ever come home?"

"Not since Dad died."

"Wow. What about my aunts?"

"Inga and her family settled in Silver Springs, Maryland. Helga never married and lives in Fort Myers, Florida."

"When was the last time you saw them?"

"Dad's funeral, not long after you were born."

Gordon asked, "Three of your siblings have Swedish first names. How did you come by your name?"

"Mom was reading a biography of George Washington on the way to the hospital the night I was born. The name Martha seemed perfect. I don't know how Harold came about."

"Maybe Grandma had been reading about the Battle of Hastings."

Although Martha had originally wanted to stay at a bed and breakfast in the center of Bath, Agnes had insisted they stay with her.

"That would be silly," said Agnes. "You know I live in a big house by myself. You grew up here."

Before going to Agnes' home, the two travelers stopped in the downtown. Mother and son hit a bookstore and a few random stores.

"I love this downtown," Martha said. "It's a great little city."

"Has it changed much since you grew up here?" asked her son.

"Not really."

"I thought you might run into some old friends."

"A lot of them, like my sisters and brothers, moved away."

"And you moved from Bath because Dad came from Tiot."

"I needed to get away. I wanted to go somewhere different. I had spent my whole life in Maine."

"And Maine used to be part of Massachusetts until 1820, so you weren't really moving to another state."

She laughed. "Kind of. Once I visited Tiot, I thought it was a good place to live. I expected to have a few children."

"Sorry to disappoint you."

"No, honey, it's just the way it worked out. I miscarried twice, so I thought I was destined to be childless. You were our miracle. Your father and I figured we'd never be parents."

Gordon smiled. "I'm glad you succeeded being a mother."

"Me, too."

They found a bakery and Gordon ordered a Pepsi... his mother, a green tea. The chocolate chip cookies looked inviting, so Martha bought two of them. They sat at a table near the window with their drinks and their treats.

A man in a blue suit approached the store. When he stepped inside the shop, he waved and exchanged salutations within several customers.

His mother gasped, almost choking on her cookie.

Gordon asked, "What's the matter?" Martha shook her head.

Their server who had blue hair yelled, "Back again, Mayor?"

Bath City Hall was located diagonally across the street.

He laughed. "It's been one of those days."

The server had quickly poured a vanilla latte in a mug. After he paid and turned to see if any of his constituents were sitting there, a smile broke out on his face.

He offered a high-wattage smile. "As I live and breathe, it's Martha McKinley."

He walked over to their table. She stood and they hugged. "My God, it's been too long. You look radiant. Who's this strapping fellow with you?"

"Curtis Bakewell, this is my son, Gordon Beckwith."

The mayor stood at five-feet nine inches tall and was still lean enough to run a mile. He had brown eyes and was tanned.

Gordon stood and shook his hand. He received a firm shake in return. "Pleasure to meet you, Gordon."

"Same here, Mayor Bakewell."

"Your mother and I went to the senior prom together a long time ago."

Gordon nodded.

"And she still looks fabulous. It must be your mother's Swedish genes." He gestured to pull up a seat. Martha nodded.

"Martha, what brings you home?" he asked. Bakewell's suit looked expensive, along with his gold watch, cuff links, and cologne.

"A visit with Mom."

"Please give her my best. She's still active in politics. She was a big help in my race for mayor. Agnes knows everything about city politics."

"That's her passion."

"Indeed."

Bakewell appraised Gordon. "You're fifteen or sixteen."

"Sixteen," replied Gordon.

"You have to be an athlete like your mother."

"Yes, my dad, too."

"Hockey?"

"Yes, and soccer in the fall."

"Good sport to get you ready for the ice. I ran cross country and track. College thoughts?"

"U-Maine. I toured it last fall. I really liked it."

"Like Mom, like son." Bakewell stood. "Unfortunately, I have to get back. Martha, great to see you. Gordon, it was a pleasure."

Bakewell waved to his server. He turned again to the Beckwiths. "If you guys are around for a few days, I'd love to take you out for supper."

Martha tried not to blush. "Curtis, thanks for the offer, but it's just a quick visit."

The mayor waved and left.

Gordon finished his cookie. "He seemed like a nice guy."

"He is." She dribbled some tea and quickly swabbed it from her face with a napkin.

"Good-looking, too."

"Yes, he is. Your father's no slouch, either." Martha wiped crumbs off their table. "Let me take you to the Maine Maritime Museum before we go see Grandma."

Gordon and Martha spend two hours in the museum with its 20-acre campus built on the Pevney and Small shipyard. They stepped out of the museum and toured the blacksmith shop and other buildings. Gordon felt something as they overlooked the Kennebec River where they found a tableau depicting Benedict Arnold's expedition stopping on the river in Bath. That sent a shiver through Gordon.

"What's the matter, Gordon?" asked his mother.

"I caught a chill off the river."

"Oh, it feels lovely."

"This is the expedition you and Dad want to trace sometime. I'm glad last fall we got to go to upstate New York to visit Saratoga."

After the museum, they drove a mile to the McKinley home on Middle Street. A woman with blonde hair opened the door as they pulled into her driveway. Agnes walked down her front steps.

Martha said, "Hi, Mom."

She rushed over to hug her mother. Gordon followed. Agnes looked up. "Martha, who is this handsome man you brought with you? Have you dumped Marty?"

Martha laughed. "It's your grandson, Gordon."

"It can't be. The Gordon I knew was a little guy the last time I saw him."

Agnes hugged him. Gordon smelled her perfume. She looked him over. "My, oh my. Gordon, it's been too long. You two come in. Supper's almost ready."

Gordon couldn't believe how his grandmother was in such good shape since she was pushing ninety. She stood erect, possessed a few wrinkles, a smattering of liver spots on her hands, and brilliant blue eyes.

The visitors sat in the dining room which featured a mahogany hutch and three windows onto the back yard.

Agnes gave Martha a coffee, and a bottle of Moxie to Gordon who looked at the bottle. "That's a fine Maine drink, Gordon. Ted Williams used to shill it. Take a sip."

Although he disdained soft drinks, Gordon tried it. "It's not bad."

She smiled and returned to the kitchen. Gordon couldn't remember the home. It seemed too big of a house for an elderly widow, but it was clean and well preserved.

The meal was simple fare consisting of roast chicken, mashed potatoes, turnip, and peas. For dessert, there was homemade blueberry pie. Gordon finished it all. After the onslaught of food, he wasn't sure if he could lift himself from the table.

Agnes spoke quickly, giving family updates, some of which Martha knew through Facebook. Her mother moved on to Bath politics.

"You ran into our new mayor."

Martha grinned. "He called you."

Agnes lifted her eyebrows. "I have my sources." She turned to Gordon. "Do you like politics?"

"A little. I love history more."

"Maine is the place for that. You already went to the maritime museum, and you drove by the Bath Iron Works where Buster worked."

"I read about Benedict Arnold spending time in Bath."

"That's right... on his ill-fated trip to Canada. It was a shame he changed sides. He was our best fighting man."

"I agree."

Agnes and Gordon continued their discussion about America's traitor while Martha brought in their bags.

Martha returned as her son helped clean up. An intense game of Scrabble ensued with Agnes edging out Martha by five points.

"You two must be pooped," said the winner. "We'll get you set up."

They walked up the stairs to the second floor. There were four bedrooms and an office. Gordon stepped into it. "That was your grandfather's hideaway, Gordon. He'd watch sports on an old black and white TV. The room still smells of his cigarettes."

She pointed to the left corner to a worn canvas bag with the name "Ross" in block letters. "That's his sea bag from the war."

There were plenty of family pictures with the parents and five siblings. Gordon took his time studying all of them. There was one picture of a young man in a Navy uniform.

Agnes pointed. "That's your grandfather at the end of the war. I love that picture. He was a good man."

"Did he talk about the war?"

"Not really. Oh, he had nightmares. Nowadays, it's called PTSD, Post Traumatic Stress Disorder. He saw a lot of action in the Pacific. He was only a little older than you when he signed up."

"I wish I had known him."

"He loved sports, mostly football, hockey, and baseball."

"Did he play when he got home?"

"Not really. He taught the boys to play, but between work and the kids, he didn't have the time to join a recreation league. When he got home from the war, he never skated again."

"That's too bad."

"Your mother says you're a good athlete and a good student."

"I try."

"Sports are great. I always loved to skate, and I try to walk every morning from here to the iron works. Achieving in school makes a big difference. Your mother was the best student of the brood. The others could've done better in school, but they were lazy. Martha wasn't. She was driven."

Agnes stepped out. Gordon looked at some more pictures and got ready for bed.

Next morning, he woke early. He heard the front door close. Looking out his window he saw Agnes step lively down the street.

He wandered over to the office, sat behind the desk and opened drawers. To Gordon's right, he saw the musty canvas bag with the name of Ross stenciled on it. The middle drawers of the desk offered old bill stubs and random slips of paper. Other drawers didn't bring up much. In the bottom right, he found under two packages of computer paper a weathered black-and-white notebook. "My War" was written on the cover. He flipped the pages. There was only a page and a half. The first few paragraphs were legible.

I was stationed as a seaman on an ugly repair ship, the U.S.S. Vestal. *Little did I know how she would have quite the history. I hadn't been aboard too long when Pearl Harbor was attacked..."*

Did he start it and never finish? Were there too many bad memories?

Buster wrote, *I hated school, so I dropped out just before graduation. I immediately walked to the Navy recruiting office on Front Street and signed up. Within a month, I was shipped to the Great Lakes Training Center in Illinois. I had never been out of Maine. I was living a great adventure. I was halfway across the country. Little did I know I would travel halfway across this planet."*

Gordon had trouble reading some of the rest. Water may have washed out some of the ink.

All of a sudden, his grandmother showed up. "You found his attempt at writing about the war years."

"You're not mad, are you?"

"No, Gordon. Martha has told me how much you love history. I'm glad you found Buster's notebook. He started writing it after he retired. I caught him at the desk with a cigarette and a beer. He told me one night, 'Honey, it's too painful. I don't know if I can go on.'"

"I told him to do what he could. His family would appreciate and cherish his memories, but he never went back to it."

Gordon put the book back into the desk drawer.

Her blue eyes misted. "I wish you had met him. He was a good man." She patted him on the shoulder. "How about some breakfast?"

Agnes stepped out and returned with a manila envelope. She handed it to her grandson. "These are a few of Buster's letters from the war he wrote to his folks. I want you to have them. You love history. It will give an insider's view to the war."

Gordon took the envelope and thanked her. His hands warmed to its touch.

~ * ~

After breakfast, the threesome drove to Boothbay Harbor, toured the town, ate lunch, and enjoyed an hour cruise of the harbor. For supper, Martha took them to the nearby Taste of

Maine Restaurant. Agnes showed Gordon how to eat lobster. Although he had never tried it, he liked it.

When they returned home, another Scrabble battle ensued. Martha outlasted her two opponents.

The next morning, they left after breakfast.

As they were leaving, Agnes hugged and kissed Gordon. "You tell your father I'm not a witch."

"I will. He did send his regards."

Martha's car needed gas. Just outside of downtown Bath, they stopped on Route 1 at a Cumberland Farms. They pulled up next to the mayor's car.

Curtis Bakewell was pumping gas when he saw Martha get out of her vehicle.

He yelled over to her, "This is a pleasant vision first thing in the morning."

She turned to see him and laughed. "No wonder you ended up as mayor. You were always a charmer."

"Look me up next time you're home."

Martha nodded.

The Beckwiths were tired and quiet throughout most of the ride. Gordon took over the driver's seat for the New Hampshire leg of the trip.

"I like Grandma. It's too bad she and Dad don't get along."

"Gordon, it boils down to two words: Curtis Bakewell. It's as simple as that, but I think Grandma has finally recovered from the shock of me marrying Marty Beckwith."

Five

Jack's Summer Job

Jack Quincy wasn't a friend of Gordon Beckwith's. He used to hang out with Gordon's one-time nemesis, Buddy LaFleur, but Jack and Buddy drifted apart starting in the ninth grade. Buddy started to hang out with the older guys on the football and hockey teams, and Buddy liked to drink beer. He got caught at the start of sophomore year. His foolishness got him suspended from the football team for four games, almost half the season. Jack and Buddy played as starting linemen on the team. Buddy tried to get Jack to go to parties. Buddy's dad, Captain Pierre LaFleur of the Massachusetts State Police, lit into his son about his suspension from the team and grounded him for two months.

"C'mon, there'll be plenty of beer. Several kegs," he told Jack.

"No, Buddy, you'll get caught again. My dad will kick my ass if I do."

Buddy laughed. "Mine will too, but I won't get caught. He works as police liaison for the district attorney, and there have been a bunch of cases. He's hardly home."

Jack shook his head. "I'm not going to risk it."

"Suit yourself. You'll miss out. There will be girls there, too."

"Buddy, you were busted for drinking last year, and you almost got booted from the football team."

"Hey, it was only four games."

"Your father wasn't happy. Do you want to get in trouble again?"

Buddy laughed. "I won't. He's super busy."

Jack walked away. Not that Jack hadn't a problem with partying and girls. Unlike Buddy, he was a serious student. His master plan was to get a scholarship to college. His father, Bradley, worked as a physical therapist and made decent money to support his two sons, but he knew he could only afford to cover the bill at a state school, not a private one. Besides, Jack's brother Ray was two years behind him and was dreaming of college as well.

Jack missed his mother, Charlene, who had worked as a nurse at Tiot Hospital. She had died from breast cancer just before he started high school. His dad could cook, but Mom had been even better. Jack loved his mother's laugh. It had rocked the house. Despite a tiring work week, her family always refreshed her.

Dad was a different person, more serious, less prone to laughter. His father loomed over his petite wife. Jack was a little afraid of his father. He had darker black skin than Jack and his coal black eyes offered a hint of menace to the world, but Bradley Quincy was an even-tempered guy. Not that he would hit his son, but still, Jack didn't want to disappoint him.

Bradley asked his oldest, "What's up for the summer?"

"Football starts in August."

Bradley stood two inches shorter than his son but was more muscular. "That leaves June, July, and part of August open."

"I'll be running and lifting getting ready for camp."

"I know that, and I commend your dedication. Other guys might slack off during the off-season, but I think it's time for you to go to work."

"Work?" asked Jack.

"Yes, that thing that pays the bills, gives us shelter, provides food, and clothes us. It's what your mother did, and I do."

"I really want to get a football scholarship."

"I know you do, son. Besides that, you possess a fine mind. You also can cover your bets for college by obtaining academic scholarships. Keep playing ball, keep studying. It will pay off."

"You always say, 'A healthy body is a healthy mind.'"

"Correct. You have to start thinking of your future."

"Do you have something in mind?"

"I do. Do you remember a classmate of mine, Clint Meadows?"

"He's come by a few times. Seemed like a good guy."

"He is. He owns a sports physical therapy center in Charlestown. I asked him about you, and he said he can definitely use you."

"To do what?" snapped Jack. "I'm sorry, Dad, I didn't mean that way." Jack took a breath. "What would I do?"

"Whatever Mr. Meadows tells you." His father generated a rare belly laugh.

"Great."

"Listen, you'll probably help clean up after patients, maybe help to lift them, and move equipment. You'll see what your old man does during the course of his work day."

"I know what you do."

"But have you really seen what I do working with folks with various ailments? Every client has different needs, different issues. We're nursing them back to good health."

Jack considered this. "Okay, I'm in. How do I get there?"

"Commuter rail to South Station and walk to the North End. If the weather's crummy, you can get off the train earlier at Back Bay and catch the subway to the T.D. Bank Garden."

"Why can't I work at your place?"

"You don't need me around. Plus, you'll get into the routine of going off to work."

"Just like you do."

"I lived on the T for school and later for work," said his dad. "You'll be responsible for getting yourself up and getting to work on time. Are we straight?"

"Yes, Dad. When?'

"The first Monday after school is ended."

Great, thought Jack. *I'm a working man. I was hoping to get some serious sack time, some relaxation, play video games, and prepare for football.*

Six

Lizzie

Unlike last year, Lizzie Soares was looking forward to spending her summer in Boston with dad Gary. Last summer, she envisioned working at the Market Basket, a short ride over the Cape Cod Canal, but her parents got her a job as an intern at the State House. She had liked staying in Boston and her co-workers, so this summer she was excited to return.

During the school year, she saw her father at her hockey games and stayed with him on weekends and during the holidays. Junior year flew by with classes and sports. She and her mother, Irene, had spent several fall weekends touring various colleges. Lizzie was still looking at pre-med, so the duo visited Johns Hopkins in Maryland, Columbia in New York City, Brown in Providence, Harvard, and Boston University. Her parents assured her they would cover her college costs, but they agreed any kind of athletic or academic scholarship to a state school would help to ease their financial burden. Between her class rank and her prowess as a hockey goalie, she had received offers from other colleges and universities. She considered going undergraduate to the University of Massachusetts before advancing to a top-notch, expensive medical school.

As busy as she was, Lizzie accepted a few dates during the year, but none progressed into a long-term relationship. She went to the junior prom with a friend, so she was a free agent heading into the summer before her senior year. She and Gordon Beckwith exchanged occasional texts, but that was the extent of that. She wondered if he was the same guy as last summer. Hopefully, Gordon would return as intern at the secretary of state's office, but she had a feeling he had moved on.

She had bugged her mother about buying a car.

"Maybe in the fall," Mom replied. "You can drive Dad's car when you're staying in Boston."

"That way you don't have to drive me to Dad's. You'll have more time with your buddy. Shouldn't I have a car for my senior year?"

"You can always take the bus."

Lizzie curled her lips. "I'm like the only upperclassman on the bus. It's all freshmen and sophomores. All my friends drive to school."

"Lizzie dear, financially, I can't afford even a good used car. I can barely keep up with our monthly expenses. Plus, your father and I want you to go to a good college."

Lizzie frowned. Her mother put an arm around her daughter.

"Work on your father. He'd do anything for you. He has a good friend who has a used car dealership in Kingston. Maybe that guy could get you a good deal."

"Okay, I'll try Dad when he's not chasing bimbos."

"You might be surprised."

"By what?"

"Is he sick?"

"No, no, I think he has a steady gal pal now. So, he may have cut down on his skirt-chasing."

"Do you know who she is?"

"She's a lawyer."

"That's no surprise."

"But I think she may have been appointed a judge."

"Hmm. Hopefully, I'll meet her."

Her mother frowned. Irene hadn't told her only child she was considering getting remarried. Lizzie wasn't a fan of her boyfriend, a fellow teacher at Sandwich High School.

Irene considered her situation with her daughter. *How would Lizzie take my getting remarried? She knows her father and I will never reconcile. Even if Lizzie dislikes this man, he treats me much better and makes me happy. I will wait a little longer before I present my case, but he's pushing me to move in together. That would send Lizzie over the edge into the Cape Cod Canal.*

Seven

Summer in the Summer

Despite her first name, Summer Atkins hated summer. Maybe not hated. She preferred New England's harsh winters. Skating, skiing, and snowboarding excited her no end. She skied on her high school team. She had studied ice dancing since she was young, quitting only a year ago.

Summer usually had spent her summers in Maine with her mother while dad toiled during the week. He would drive up after work every Friday.

Summer didn't totally hate the warm weather. Her family owned a summer home in Wells, Maine, and she enjoyed her time at Moody Beach, but UV rays weren't kind to her fair skin. She never tanned; sunshine only reddened her. Her blonde hair brightened in the sun; her freckle quota expanded on her face.

But hard times had changed her family's life. Her father, Barry, lost his job as the IT manager at a biotech firm in Cambridge while her mother, Melody, taught kindergarten, and painted kitchens and bathrooms in the summer. Bills had multiplied, so to cope with the rising debt, her parents debated selling the Wells house. She was devastated.

With the painting jobs piling up, Melody had to stay home to work. The family time in Maine had diminished.

Barry Atkins stepped into his daughter's bedroom as she was finishing her homework.

She swiveled in her chair to face him. "Hey, Dad, what's up?'

He looked at her eyes which were glassy from the joint she'd been smoking earlier.

"Honey, you're going to have to work this summer. You're sixteen, and you can't be hanging around."

"I would've been hanging out in Wells, but we rented out the house for the summer."

"Summer, do you think we wanted to do that? We just moved into this house two years ago, and we have a large monthly mortgage bill. I love the Wells place as much you. It will kill Mom and me to have to get rid of it."

"You couldn't put that off until next year?"

"Ideally, yes. Financially, I don't think so."

Summer frowned. "Great, no Wells, and I have to work."

"Despite that, we expected you to start working at sixteen. We all did."

"Yeah, yeah, and you walked barefoot to school in ten-foot snowdrifts."

He laughed. "They were at least fifteen-feet high."

Barry paused. "Working looks good on a college app."

She slapped her forehead. "Oh, do I have to go to a cheaper college now?"

"No, you are covered in a trust your late grandmother set up years ago. Even when you were born, my mother knew a good education was going to cost a lot of dollars."

"Thank goodness for that. I thought I'd have to apply to Middlesex Community College."

"Your fears are unfounded in that matter. Until I get back on my feet, we have to stay ahead of our creditors."

Summer scratched her head. "Where should I apply for a job? Supermarket? Walmart? I can see myself at the front of the store as the official greeter. 'My name is Summer. Welcome to Walmart.'"

"You'd be a great greeter, but I do have a summer job in mind. One of my former co-workers, Dick Bentley, has a friend who runs the *Constitution* Museum in Charlestown, and they have an intern program."

"Oh great, I'll be the official greeter at the *Constitution*. 'Hi, my name is Summer. Welcome aboard the *U.S.S. Constitution*.'"

"You'd work in the museum, not on the ship. That's still part of the Navy."

"Dad, you dragged me there a long time ago. I thought it was smelly."

"There's a World War Two destroyer next to *Old Ironsides*."

"Yes, we went on that, too. BORING!"

"This would look great on a college app."

She paced her room. "You might have a point. I don't have to like it."

"Mom or I would drop you at the commuter rail which would take you to North Station, and it's a short walk to the Navy Yard."

"Hmm. I'll have my license soon. It would be a change of scenery. I'd go into Boston."

"You'd be near the North End with all its great restaurants. You love Italian food. Maybe Mom and I would meet you for supper after work."

She nodded. "I do love the North End; I do love Italian food. Okay, Dad, you sure you weren't into sales instead of IT?"

"I would've been an awful salesman. I'd rather hunker over a computer monitor."

"Could you get a job there for Cyrus?" Barry was no fan of Summer's boyfriend.

Barry laughed. "Really? That would be great... the two of you smoking weed on the *Constitution*?"

"I don't smoke."

"Really? I've smelled it on you several times, Summer. You look stoned right now. Does Cyrus go to class high?"

"He only smokes to relax. Dad, if Cyrus worked with me, we could carpool. He has his license."

"I know he's a year older than you."

"He gets good grades."

"He doesn't seem extremely motivated. What kind of guy wears shorts all year round?"

"Cold doesn't bother him. You don't like him because he's not a jock. He's into flowers and nature," answered Summer. "Maybe he could be like Bill Gates, drop out of school, and create his own startup."

"Good for him, but I'm lucky I got you the job. I'm not going to recommend Cyrus, a white guy with dreadlocks who reeks of reefer."

"He doesn't reek."

"Summer, you must've lost your sense of smell. If cannabis could be turned into cologne, he could start his own fragrance line."

Summer's face grew pinker. "You've never liked him."

"I've never said that. I just couldn't see the attraction. That's all."

"He's a good guy."

"I think there are better ones out there."

"We've gone out for two years. He's faithful."

"Well, good for him. He's got that going for him."

Summer bent over, picked up a small pillow, and threw it at her father. She missed.

"Nice arm, honey."

"Are you really my father?"

"I'd be happy to have my mouth swabbed if you don't believe me."

She sniffled. "Close the door on the way out."

Barry grinned.

Summer wasn't happy about her prospects. She texted Cyrus about the plan.

He responded, "Bummer, babe."

Eight

Victor

Victor Santos' mother, Victoria, wanted her son to stay off the streets. Several of his friends were headed for trouble.

Victor is too smart to join a gang, she said to herself. *Well, I hope he will be intelligent, not be a follower.*

Victoria worked as an emergency room nurse at the Carney Hospital in Dorchester's Lower Mills neighborhood. They lived on a quiet street five minutes away; ambulances and police and fire sirens could be heard occasionally.

She always had directed Victor toward sports, especially basketball and baseball, and there her only child thrived. If he weren't so lackadaisical in school, Victor could excel in the classroom. He didn't want any of his friends to consider him smart.

"You can do better in school, Victor," she said. "Good grades and sports will help you go to a good college."

"I don't know if I want to go to college, Mom."

"What?" she shrieked. She slapped him on the back of the head. "What're you going to do for work?"

"Skinny Graham told me he could get me in his uncle's steelworker union. It's good pay."

"And hard work. Is that what you want? To bust your ass instead of using your mind?"

Victor shrugged. "Skinny and me would work together. We'd be outside instead of being behind a desk."

"Do you ever see those guys out humping during the cold weather?"

"Yuh, but they're bundled up."

"You're the guy who hates winter who wants to work out in the cold?"

"Not a problem."

She laughed. "Victor, you're a bad liar. For starters, we have to get you a job for the summer."

"I thought I would hang out with my boys."

"I don't think so. That will only land you in trouble."

"My friends aren't gangsters."

"Right now, but what if the allure of easy money turns them into bad guys?"

"We know who the bad dudes are. They're cool."

Victoria shook her head. "I have a friend at the Carney whose sister works at the state library in Boston. They usually have a few high school kids working there, and I'm going to ask about you."

"Me work in a library? That's for girls."

"Plenty of guys work in libraries."

"Not many."

"Nonetheless, I think you would like it. You're a reader. Your friends think you only live for sports, video games, comics, and girls. I know differently about all the books and sketch pads in your bedroom."

Victor frowned. He left his mother for his room.

I don't want to work in a stupid library. Skinny will laugh at me.

Victor stared at his crowded bookcase. He walked over and picked up *The Stand* by Stephen King. He had read it twice already. Thoughts of the summer job crowded his mind, so King's words tumbled without any meaning.

Victor's library consisted of mostly horror and fantasy novels. They took him away from the daily existence of living in the city. He would love to write books of this genre. Lately, he had started to scribble in an old school notebook. Victor had no real plots, but he wrote down ideas on characters and what kind of worlds they might live in.

Victor's English teacher at Cathedral High School, Mrs. Lydia Fontanez, had told him he was a good writer. She had taught at the school for twenty years.

Last fall, she stood outside the gymnasium door near the bus stop on Washington Street and grabbed him as school was ending for the day.

Victor and Skinny walked by her. She hailed Victor. "A word." Skinny slipped past him.

"Victor," she said, "you can write. You know that."

He nodded. He hoped nobody else had seen him talking with her besides Skinny.

"You know what revise means?"

"Yes."

"After you write something, look it over. Read it out loud. Check your spelling, check your punctuation. Does the writing sound like your voice? All good writers revise their work."

"Yes, Mrs. Fontanez."

"You could be an A student. Don't settle for Bs and Cs." She looked over at Skinny. "That goes for you as well, Royce." Unlike other teachers, Mrs. Fontanez refused to call him Skinny.

She always tried to reach out to her students. Many times, she was ignored, but she always tried.

The two friends crossed Washington Street for the bus stop.

Skinny knew of Victor's interest in books and drawing. He also enjoyed those kinds of movies and TV shows with superheroes, magic, or horror. Although Skinny wasn't big on reading books, he devoured comic books.

Victor's mother worked hard to provide for them. She had sworn off men. Victor was her world. He was happy they had their own home. Many of his friends lived in loud, crowded apartments. Victoria received many dating offers, but she turned them all down.

When he stepped off the trolley on the Mattapan/Milton line, Victor shuffled to his house. When he got there, he grabbed the empty trash and recycling barrels from the end of the driveway and took them into the garage.

They lived in a white Cape Cod house with black shutters and a small, enclosed backyard. In the good weather, Victor loved to grab a chair, put on his earbuds, close his eyes, and listen to music. Today, his notebook rested in his lap.

He wondered who his father was. If he were alive, where was he right now? Did he know he had a son? If he did, did he even ever care about his child? *If I was a dad, I wouldn't ignore my kid.*

Why don't I know who he is? Why won't Mom tell me who he is? Were we not good enough for him?

His mother never mentioned him. For all she cared, Victor's father could die a horrible death or go to hell. Either way worked for her.

Nine

Abbie's First Job

Abbie Fortune chuckled to herself.

I'm alone on a Saturday night while my mother is out on a date. How weird is that? Should I stay up for her? Will she be late? Would she not come home? That would be really crazy.

Claudia Gomes (no more Fortune after the divorce) hadn't seen her ex-husband Jack for five years, then he pulled a Lazarus and returned. She thought she loved him, but she feared him relapsing into his gambling addiction and putting her and Abbie into debt. Jack tried to rekindle their relationship, but she had turned him down every time. Sure, they spent family time with Abbie, but Claudia didn't spend any alone time with him. Jack had worked hard to stay in shape and resurrect his athletic shape through biking, but it didn't make her look twice.

Being a single parent and sole breadwinner for a long time had been easy for her. Claudia never felt like she was missing out.

Her former boss at the library tried to woo her to no avail. She ended up succeeding him as the director of the Folkstone Library.

Since last year, she had started seeing Secretary of State Mark Preston. He was a bachelor politician who might become the governor of Massachusetts. Despite her wariness about pols, she was very comfortable in his company. As the director of the state library, Claudia's office stood a stone's throw from the secretary of state's. They saw each other almost on a daily basis, but they kept their relationship to themselves. They would run into each other in the halls of the State House and chat. The two of them reunited almost every Saturday, which was becoming her favorite day of the week.

Even though her father, Jack, had remarried to a coworker and was about to become a dad again, Abbie loved him and was happy for him with his wife, Theresa. She was more excited for her mother who was happier than she'd been in a long time. She liked Mark Preston and wondered if someday he might become her stepfather.

Holy crap, she said to herself. *Mark could become my stepfather. Wow! And from my stepmom, I might have a little brother or sister. It was simpler when it was just me and Mom.*

After she ate dinner, Abbie texted with her friend Ramona Ramirez, also her soccer teammate. Then she made tea and searched through her DVDs and Blu-rays for a movie. Abbie picked *Sleepless in Seattle*. Ensconced in a lounge, she sipped her tea. Unfortunately, she missed Tom Hanks and Meg Ryan finally meeting at the top of the Empire State Building and awoke to the end credits. She turned off the player and the TV and wondered if she should get ready for bed.

At midnight, her mother waltzed in.

Abbie said in a serious tone, "And where have you been, young lady? It's getting late." She tapped her wristwatch. "It's almost morning."

Claudia hugged her daughter. "I was out having a good time. Am I grounded?"

Abbie laughed. "I'll think about it."

Claudia took off her jacket and hung it up. "Quiet night?"

"Texted with Ramona, drank tea, and missed the ending of *Sleepless*."

"You could rewind it."

"I know. I'm tired now. I'm going to head in."

"Okay." Abbie started down the hall. "I can get you a job at the State House."

"With you in the library?"

"Possibly. Mark wanted to know if you wanted to be a summer intern."

"Like Gordon?"

"Yes. That way you wouldn't be with me the whole work day. We'd just commute together."

"Can I think about it?"

"Gordon seemed to like working there."

"Yeah, he did." Would that have been strange working every day with Gordon?

"But he's not going back?"

"I think he had another tunnel experience at the State House."

"Really?" Claudia had experienced Gordon's touch with the past.

"So he wanted to do something else. Be far away from tunnels."

"Let me know tomorrow so I can tell Mark Monday when I go to work."

"Sure. Good night."

Claudia kissed her daughter on the cheek.

Ten

The Boss Man

"Am I going to have to deal with spoiled teenagers again this summer?" Benny Goodman asked no one in particular. "They're totally useless. They're always on their phones and not paying attention to the task at hand."

Goodman had worked at the museum for a decade. His assistant, Emma Wollensky, silently laughed at his annual rant about the summer help.

"Benny, they're not all bad," she said, pulling her tea bag out of her mug. "You've had a few good ones. Some went on to major in history. They were inspired working here, soaking up all this history."

"What good did that do them?"

"Maybe, they shared the newly discovered love of history with others. Maybe, they went into teaching; maybe, they went into research. Doesn't somebody I know have a Ph.D. from Harvard in U.S. History?"

"What good did that do me besides building up a lot of loans?"

"You work at a museum at one of the great national parks in the country, a fabulous piece of history. Where else do you want to be?"

Goodman shook his head. "I don't know, Emma. Maybe, I had a different vision for myself."

"What? You wanted a tenured professorship at Harvard or Oxford?" She poured a little milk in her mug, added sugar, and stirred. She sipped. "How is your book coming?"

He smirked. "It's coming. *A History of the Boston Navy Yard and its Role in America's History.*"

"So?"

"Slow."

"Have you finished your research?"

"Pretty much." Benny sat at his desk and stared out the window.

"Have you started writing it?"

"Sort of."

"How many pages?"

"I can't get past the first chapter. I was thinking of a prologue to hook the reader in."

"That sounds good. Have you written it?"

"Sort of. I don't have a comfortable draft."

Emma took another sip and exhaled. "You've been at it since I've been here."

"I'm a slow writer."

"Are you blocked?"

"Just distracted."

Emma knew a major source of his distraction: his divorce five years earlier. His wife, Tovah, had left him for the wife of one of his college friends. He couldn't believe his wife left him for another woman. He knew that he wasn't out of the ordinary in the 21st-century, but it hurt his male ego. Benny would've been happier if she had left him for another guy. That he could understand, but not for Patty O'Connell, whom Benny had dated for two years at Harvard before Tovah. Patty dumped him for a Cambridge cop whom she married and later divorced. Patty and Tovah opened an art studio in Rockport. Benny wanted to check it out, but the thought sickened him.

Emma pointed her gold-and-black Boston Bruins mug at him. "Maybe you'll be more motivated with the good weather."

"Maybe."

Benny was worried about the next board of trustees meeting. He couldn't shake off his feelings of inadequacy. He was forty-two, divorced, and childless. Tovah had assured him they would have children, but they had no success with that. Looking back, children hadn't been a priority for her. Although about half of his friends got divorced, most of them had kids.

When he got home to his condo in Somerville, there wasn't much to do. He had played drums and sang in a four-piece band with occasional wedding gigs, but he quit after the divorce. Although his famous namesake played clarinet, Benny preferred percussion. He loved rock 'n roll. His parents loved classical music, which he abhorred. He only got any recognition from his parents when he joined the marching band at Newton South High School. He had to practice the drums when they went out shopping. His mother complained his drumming kicked up her migraines.

"Benny, please, stop that racket!" she'd yell. "My head is splitting."

Sometimes he'd whack the drums louder just to aggravate her.

His parents were proud of his academic achievements. Unfortunately, they died before he graduated from Harvard. Mom and Dad had loved cigarettes; Benny preferred beer.

His older sister, Mindy, lived with her family in Syracuse, and they only connected intermittently.

Benny wondered how long this morning's hangover would last.

Eleven

Jack's New Fortune

Theresa Fortune timed her contractions. In their bed, she nudged her husband who was unaware of the imminent birth.

"Jack, time to go." She poked him in the ribs.

"Huh? What?"

"Time to go."

"Go? Oh! Gotcha."

In advance of the big day, Theresa had packed her bag for the hospital. Both got dressed quickly. They climbed into their SUV and headed for delivery at Newton-Wellesley Hospital. It wasn't the closest facility, but friends of Theresa's raved about the care.

They left Raynham and took Route 24 north to the hospital.

"How you feeling, Jack? Are you excited?"

"I am."

"You seem a little nervous."

"Maybe. It's been a while."

She punched him on the right arm. "I'm doing the heavy lifting. You're just the coach and the chauffeur."

Theresa moaned softly.

Jack turned briefly. "You okay?"

"The contractions are coming quickly."

"Will we make it?"

"Not unless you give it more gas."

They left Route 24 and turned north onto Route 128. Because it was early morning, the usual traffic hadn't occurred. As he sped, Jack looked at the dashboard. Time: 4:34 a.m.

He couldn't remember being up that early. Jack felt drops of sweat trickling down his back.

Will I be a good father? Will I be a good provider? Am I too old for an infant?

Theresa looked at him. "You will be fine, Jack. I see your brain on fire. You'll do great. It's our child. Abbie will have a little brother or sister."

"I wonder how she'll feel, Theresa."

"Abbie's a mature girl, wiser than her years. How will Claudia take it?"

"Claudia's having the time of her life. She really hasn't given me much thought since I took off."

"Do you blame her?"

"No, I don't, but I had to leave to protect them."

"They know that."

She groaned. "If you ever start gambling, you'll be out on your ass. I'm not the cultured lady like your ex. I'm a tough little bitch. If you hurt me, I'll hurt you."

Sweat drenched Jack. "I believe you, honey."

She laughed and shuddered at the same time. "As long you understand me. I plan on the long haul with you and whoever this is."

They made it to Newton. Jack pulled up in front of the emergency room. An attendant came out with a wheelchair and pushed Theresa inside. Jack parked inside the garage and hustled to maternity.

Thirty minutes later, Manual John Fortune, eight pounds, two ounces, was born. Jack couldn't believe it. A son. Tears dripped down his cheeks.

Little later, Jack called his daughter. "Abbie, you have a brother."

"That's great, Dad. You and Theresa must be ecstatic."

"We are, Abbie. We are. I just hope to be a better father."

"You will, Dad. You will."

Abbie ended the call silently laughing that she had a little brother, much younger than her. Unlike her life, Abbie hoped young Manny wouldn't suffer five years of his life without a father.

Claudia shrugged when she was told the baby news.

Abbie wondered when her father would take her out for her driving lessons.

"Your dad sells cars," said Claudia Fortune. "He'll take you out to drive when he has time away from dealing with an infant."

"I hope he can spare the time."

Claudia smiled. "With a newborn in his house, he may want to occasionally escape for a drive with an untested teenager."

Twelve

Emma Wollensky

    Emma Wollensky loved hockey. No one else in her family did. She had grown up in Melrose, north of Boston. Her two older brothers, Stephen and Jack, played basketball. Her father, Sam, and her mother, Madeline, weren't sports nuts, yet they caught as many of the children's games as they could. Her parents encouraged her skating. She joined her first girls' hockey team when she was ten. She played in high school and at Harvard. She had dreams of playing for Team USA. That dream ended with a leg injury. Emma still played in a night co-ed pickup league. Fortunately, she was a good student, finishing in the top ten at Melrose High School. She landed her job at the *Constitution* Museum after originally working as a summer intern. When she graduated from Harvard with a history degree, Benny Goodman hired her. Within a few years, she had worked her way up to her current position. Benny encouraged Emma to seek her master's, but Emma wasn't sure. Even though her parents owned a successful jewelry store, she still carried the responsibility for her student debt.

Her brothers appreciated their parents' hard work and dedication to their store, but it wasn't the life for them. Stephen went to Bentley College while Jack studied at Bryant University. Both brothers worked and thrived for Fidelity.

Stephen told her several times, "Emma, Jack and I can get you into Fidelity. You'll start at the bottom and work your way up. Get your MBA and earn good money."

Each time she declined. Money would be great, but she wouldn't be stimulated or happy. History and sports got her excited. Her parents helped to defray a chunk of her tuition, so she commuted to Harvard instead of living on the grounds of America's oldest university.

At twenty-eight, Emma wasn't sure what her dream job was. She loved the museum, but she considered teaching, coaching, and sports writing. She mentioned the latter to her parents, who dissuaded her of the notion.

After a Sunday supper with her parents, Sam said, "They get paid squat. You'd have to start at the bottom at a newspaper or at a place like ESPN. Is that what you want?"

"Maybe, Dad."

"Go back to school and get your master's. At the very least, if you go into teaching, you'd get paid more than someone with just a bachelor's degree."

"I still have my loans for Harvard. I don't know if I want fresh debt."

"You're making good money at the museum. Get your master's online or at night and weekends."

"It would be tough doing that while working at the museum."

And it would cut into her time for hockey.

"You could do it. Your brothers have their MBAs."

After college graduation, Stephen and Jack had headed straight to grad school at Babson College.

Her mother didn't condemn her dreams. "Emma, you do what makes you happy. Your father and your brothers love you and support you, and only want what's best for you. But you chart your own course. I wanted to write or to teach English. Your father opened the store, we had babies, and I started helping out when I could. Dreams were deferred."

"When the business got better, you could've stepped away."

Her mother smiled. "Probably, Emma, but by then, I enjoyed working there, handling our customers, and I'm a better salesperson than your father."

Emma laughed. "You're right. He's a great manager, but you have a connection with the customers. Dad would suffer if you stepped away."

Emma shared her mother's expertise with the store stock and her way with customers. Her parents always encouraged her to do her own thing. Although they never said it out loud, she suspected they wanted her to take over the reins of the business when they eventually stepped away. Her brothers were comfortable in their own careers and ignored the family business as much as possible. They offered financial advice to sell the store when they retired. The siblings weren't going to follow in their footsteps.

Emma wanted to follow her own path, not her brothers', nor her parents'.

Thirteen

The Docent

Ten years ago, when his wife Doris died, Mitchell Ledowski didn't know what to do with himself. Sure, he could hang out at the American Legion, but he didn't like to drink. He could hang out at the local senior center, but a lot of old people assembled there. Even though he had just turned seventy, he didn't feel geriatric. He could get a job bundling groceries at Market Basket, but that didn't entice him either. Mitch even considered substitute teaching, but after thirty-eight years in the classroom, enough was enough.

His only child, Sally Ledowski O'Neil, called her father every day after her mother passed away from dementia. Sally had three children, so she couldn't afford to allow grief to consume her like her dad did, although she missed her mom as much as her dad missed his wife. Despite her busy life working as a real estate attorney and keeping up her home, Sally made sure to stay in touch with Mitch even though he lived twenty minutes away.

Mitch had occupied his time going to daily Mass and walking the streets of Winthrop, a seaside town bordering East Boston and Revere. Other than two years in the U.S. Navy, he had spent his entire life in that town. Despite its proximity to Boston, he felt Winthrop possessed a small-town charm. There were only two accessible ways in and out of it—Saratoga Street in Eastie or Revere St. to Revere. Logan Airport was situated within an arm's reach. Once you got used to the sounds of planes landing and taking off, you were fine. Mitch loved to walk and catch the views of Boston Harbor and the Atlantic Ocean. He never got sick of it.

He knew Sally was worried about him and his health. Although he had passed his last physical exam with flying colors. When Doris got sick, he learned to cook, clean the house, and wash and iron their clothes. He became self-sufficient.

One time after he had cooked chicken piccata for the two of them, Sally said, "You'd make a great partner with all your domestic skills. This chicken piccata is fabulous."

He laughed. "One marriage is enough. I can't believe folks like Elizabeth Taylor or Mickey Rooney getting married a bunch of times."

"You and Mom had a great marriage and were great parents."

"We tried for more children, but we lost two. We were sad you were an only child."

"I never felt sad. You and Mom were good company. I had plenty of friends."

She stirred her pasta. "Dad, you need an outlet."

"You mean a hobby? I do modelling."

"Dad, I was down in the cellar recently. You have an unfinished model of the U.S.S. *Constitution*."

"I'm working on it."

She chuckled. "There was so much dust and cobwebs. I used Pledge on it. If the ship builders had to wait for you, *Old Ironsides* would never have gotten launched."

"You're right, honey. Once Mom got sick, I didn't have the time. Now, I'm not in the mood."

"You just can't be moping around Winthrop. At least take a ride and walk Revere Beach for a change. Get a hot dog at Kelly's Roast Beef. You got us out on the weekends. We drove up and down the coast. We went to Salem, Marblehead, Ipswich, Newburyport, Portsmouth, and Kittery. And you'd give us some history of each place. You wouldn't tell Mom or me where we were headed. You'd say, 'The Ledowskis are going out for an adventure.' Granted, for the most part, they were day trips, but we knew you'd make a big deal out of it."

He sipped his coffee. Sally grinned. "I loved to go riding with you guys. We used to bring some of my friends. They'd say, 'Sally, can we come on one of your adventures?' They claimed they never went anywhere with their folks. They were jealous, and I was proud they wanted to tag along."

"I think your friend, Margie Livermore, was a frequent flyer on our trips. I haven't thought about her for years. What is she doing?"

"She's married and lives in Swampscott. She works as an attendant for Jet Blue. After our adventures, she wanted to see more of the world, and she has."

Mitch smiled. "She's probably had a lot more adventures than we had."

"We talk occasionally or we text."

"Please give her my regards."

"I will. Back to you, Dad. You need that outlet."

"When you find it, let me know."

After gelato for dessert, he washed up, and she dried. After Sally put away the last dish, the idea hit her.

"I've got it, Dad!" She folded the dish towel and looped it around the stove handle.

"What?"

"You can be a guide at the Navy Yard. You served in the Navy. You taught history; you'd be perfect. Every day you would meet all kinds of people. You'd be a natural."

"They probably have enough volunteers."

"Fiddlesticks. You served on that destroyer there."

"Yes, the U.S.S. *Cassin Young.*"

"You know what it was like to serve on such a ship."

"I was lucky to serve without coming under fire."

"I'm going to call and find out. Do you think it's a good idea?"

He pursed his lips. "Maybe."

"Dad, it's in Charlestown, practically in your back yard. Maybe seeing *Old Ironsides* will get you to finally finish the model of her I gave you a few years ago."

"Sally, you are a pushy person. You remind me of someone I know."

"Mom. She said we were a lot alike."

Sally followed through with her idea, and her father started as a docent, or guide, at the Navy Yard, welcoming visitors aboard the destroyer. He worked five days a week and looked forward to it every day.

~ * ~

Ten years had passed. His health stayed in good shape for his age as he had just turned eighty.

He was talking to Benny Goodman in mid-June about summer interns.

"Hello, Mr. Goodman," Mitch hailed from the ship.

"Mitch, please call me Benny."

"Mr. Goodman, you're the man. I respect you."

Benny laughed. Mitch Ledowski was one of his favorite people around the place. He loved working as a docent on the *Cassin Young* and occasionally filled in at the *Constitution*. Benny thought Mitch knew more about history than he did, even with his doctorate.

"Mitch, we're going to have a couple of summer interns. Can I send them to you for a tour of the ship?"

"Absolutely."

"You have a great day, Mitch."

"You, too, Mr. Goodman."

Benny chuckled to himself and headed to his building. Mitch made him smile in spite of his own surliness.

Fourteen

Opening Day Departures

Gordon got up at six, ate breakfast, showered, jumped on his bike, and arrived early for the train to Boston. He barely said hello and goodbye to his parents. Marty and Martha looked at each other and smiled after his rapid departure.

Abbie Fortune was excited to work in Boston, even if it was for a job arranged by her mother's boyfriend, Mark Preston. She rose early, got ready, ate breakfast, and rode with her mom to the station. The two of them walked to the platform where Abbie saw a familiar figure, reading a book and carrying his black Boston Bruins backpack—Gordon Beckwith.

Claudia said, "You can go with Gordon. I've got stuff to review."

"Hi, stranger," Abbie said.

Gordon looked up from a large biography of Ulysses S. Grant. "Hey, Abbie. You're working in town?"

"At your old job. You're headed for the Navy Yard."

"Yes. Please say hi to Doc Ott for me. He's a good guy."

"Do you wish you were going back?"

"I liked the people, but I needed a change."

Abbie knew Gordon's penchant for finding secret tunnels had reemerged the prior summer at the State House.

~ * ~

Jack Quincy wasn't an early riser. His father always had to shake him multiple times. Alarms never roused Jack. In the winter, his father would pull off his covers. Only then would the drop in the temperature in the bed wake up his son.

"Get a move on, buddy," said Jack. "You have to get up for work."

"Ah, c'mon."

"Welcome to the real world."

Jack shuffled to the bathroom and performed all his duties. He appeared at the breakfast table with his brother, Ray.

Afterwards, they drove to Tiot Depot. "You have money, lunch, and your phone?" asked Dad.

"Yup."

"Don't be so happy."

"I'm going to work nights when I get older."

"Good luck with that, Jack. Be good. Do what they tell you. You're a reflection not only of yourself, but of your parents. Your mom would have been proud of you. Okay?"

"Okay," muttered Jack. He wondered what his mother would think of her oldest son going off to his first job. He missed her badly and dreamed of her.

"Have a great day. I'll see you for supper."

"How will I get home from the station?"

"In this country it's called walking."

"Can't wait to get my license."

"I can. See you."

Jack noticed there were a lot of people waiting for the train. He hadn't taken the train since he was little when his parents had taken him to the aquarium and the Children's Museum. He wished his mom were there.

The night before, his father had shown him how to work the ticket app. He wasn't sure where to stand. All of a sudden, he saw someone waving at him and calling his name.

She yelled, "Jack!"

He looked and saw two familiar faces. "Abbie? Beckwith?"

Jack joined them on the platform, happy to have company on the trip.

When the train pulled in, the three classmates found a three-seater on the upper deck of the train. Gordon kept his book in his bag.

Gordon said, "Abbie's got my old job as a summer intern in the secretary of state's office."

"It helped that my mother is dating the secretary of state," chimed in Abbie.

Jack laughed. "No way, but your mom is a player. She is hot. I mean no disrespect."

"Don't worry, Jack. I've known it my whole life."

Jack felt uncomfortable. "You're hot, too, Abbie."

"Good save," said Gordon, who chortled. "Where are you off to?"

"Charlestown. I'm working at a physical rehab place. I think my dad wanted me to get a taste of his world."

Abbie asked, "Is that what he does?"

"Yup. He especially likes working with folks who have suffered bad injuries or are rehabbing after surgeries."

"That's an important job," she said. "You'd have to know all about the human body. It sounds interesting."

"Maybe. I don't expect I'll be giving out advice on how to treat a bad back. I'll probably be cleaning the bathrooms."

Gordon laughed. "I've done that, Jack. Lots of fun."

"It's a crappy job, but somebody has to do it."

The three laughed. Gordon said, "Hopefully, it will be all behind you."

Abbie slapped Gordon's arm. "That's gross."

"You laughed." Abbie grinned.

"Jack, I'm going to Charlestown," said Gordon. "The Navy Yard. I'll be a summer intern at the *Constitution* Museum."

"You're a history nerd."

Abbie smiled. "He's the nerdiest history guy."

Gordon wanted to change the subject. "Are you taking the subway from Back Bay to North Station?"

"Yes."

"Good, we'll be together, as poor Abbie walks up from South Station to the State House."

When Jack and Gordon stood up at Back Bay Station, they wished Abbie well.

When all the passengers stepped off the train, Abbie thought how great it was to have Gordon's company, as well as Jack's. She moved a few spots to sit with her mother.

I hope this job is going to work out, she thought to herself.

Jack and Gordon climbed up stairs to the main concourse at Back Bay, and then they walked down another set of stairs to wait for the Orange Line subway.

"Gordon, how come you didn't go back to your old job?" asked Jack.

An innocent question, but Gordon didn't want to tell Jack, whom he didn't know that well, why he was too spooked to return to the State House. Two years ago, Jack had experienced tunnel time with Gordon.

"Change of pace, Jack. My dad's friend mentioned the job at the Navy Yard. As a history nerd, who wouldn't want to work by *Old Ironsides* and a World War Two destroyer?"

The subway arrived and they crammed in with a score of their close and personal friends. After twenty minutes and a bunch of stops, they arrived at North Station. Gordon pointed to their left at the Boston Garden, home of the Boston Bruins and Boston

Celtics. The Garden had been the site of Gordon's last playoff hockey game.

"Maybe you'll play there for the Bruins, Gordon," said Jack.

"I'd love to, but it would take a lot of work and luck to play pro."

Jack nodded. "I think you have a shot."

"I didn't know you like hockey."

"Because I'm Black?"

"No, Jack, because I thought football was your passion."

"It is. But, c'mon, I love all sports. Hockey is something I've gotten into the last few years. I went to all the Tiot playoff games."

Once they stepped off the subway, it was a quick walk over the North Washington Street Bridge to their destination.

They saw the Navy's most famous ship painted black and white. "I guess this is me. Good luck with the bathrooms, Jack."

"Thanks, I hope it will all be behind me when I go home. Maybe see you later on the train."

"Maybe."

~ * ~

In another part of Boston, Victor Santos couldn't believe his mother had shouted, "Victor! Time to get up."

"What?" he choked out his reply.

"Time to get ready for work."

"Oh."

Victoria returned to the kitchen; her son returned to slumber land.

Ten minutes later, she came back and shook him. "Now, Victor. Into the shower."

He dragged himself to the bathroom. When he finished, his mother had laid out his clothes: a dress shirt, a tie, and a pair of chinos. This wasn't his standard code of torn jeans and a t-shirt.

"I can't wear this."

"First impressions are important. I'll tie your tie when you're ready."

After he quietly ate his breakfast, his mother, dressed in her nursing scrubs said, "You know where you're going. Right?"

"Yes, Mom. Take the bus, take the subway. I take the T every day to school."

"But you're going downtown for the summer. It's a slightly different trip."

Victor pushed his cereal bowl into the sink and ran back to brush his teeth.

Victoria made one final inspection. Her son stood a lean five feet, eight inches tall with light brown skin, thick, curly hair with blue eyes. She tied his tie.

"What a handsome guy. Stay away from the girls."

He rolled his eyes. She kissed him, and he stepped outside. As Victor headed to the bus stop, his neighbor Gus Saunders called out to him.

"Are you going to a funeral, Victor?"

Victor shuffled with his head down. "Downtown to the State House, Mr. Saunders."

"I drive right by there. Hop in." Gus drove a crimson Land Rover which always sparkled.

Victor thought it was better than dealing with public transportation. Not every rider on the T practiced personal hygiene.

He was a stocky Black man with an off-kilter long nose and a winning smile. Gus wore a blue Patriots windbreaker over his court officer uniform of white shirt, blue Trial Court patch on his shoulder, dark pants, and black shoes.

"Excited?" he asked as they slipped out of Mattapan into Dorchester.

"I guess so. I've never worked before."

"Where in the State House?"

"The library," replied Victor.

"It's a beautiful building. When I got out of the Navy, I wanted to work there instead of at the courthouse. Now here I am twenty-five years later still working in the court system."

"Do you like it?"

"Victor, some of my co-workers complain. I don't. I love working with all kinds of people—white, Black, Latino, Asian. Everybody deserves to be treated with respect and dignity. Not all my compadres feel the same."

"What do you do?"

"The job has changed a lot. When I first came on, anybody could be a court officer. Now there are requirements and lots of training."

"Really?"

"I've done classes in defensive tactics, CPR, working in the jury pool. I work sometimes in the courtroom to keep it safe. I work in the lockup where we process prisoners, I work sometimes at the main entrance checking in folks, I work sometimes with folks who come to do jury duty. It's rarely dull."

"Sounds interesting."

"I consider myself fortunate. I have my own house. It's not a mansion, but it's mine. I can go on vacations."

"You're a bachelor?"

"A long time ago, when I was stationed in San Diego, I had a wife. She died in childbirth with our son. I'm a widower."

"Do you want to get remarried?"

"Nah, I'm too set in my ways." Saunders laughed. "But I don't ignore the ladies."

They pulled up in front of the 54th Massachusetts Regiment statue across from the State House, which had been celebrated in the movie, *Glory*.

"Here we are. Have a good day, Victor."

"You, too, Mr. Saunders. Thanks for the ride."

"I get out at four-thirty. If you want a ride home, walk down the hill to the Brooke Courthouse. Ask for me, and I'll give you a ride."

"Thanks."

~ * ~

Not far from the State House, Lizzie Soares shared breakfast with her dad.

"Are you excited to be back at the State House this summer?" he asked, while buttering his toast.

"Kind of. I have a feeling there will be different interns this time."

"You liked last year's crew. Didn't you? Wasn't there a guy?"

She blushed. "Yes, but I don't think he's coming back."

"There could be another guy this year."

"Maybe. I'm not worried. I didn't really date anyone this year."

"You didn't?"

"No, Dad, junior year was tough enough between sports and studies."

Gary grinned. "Still thinking pre-med?"

"I am."

"I have a friend who's on the admissions board at Boston University Medical."

"I still have to do undergrad."

"You could go to B.U. for both."

"Dad, I might want to go out of state for undergrad. I've lived a sheltered life in Plymouth. I want to see what's out there."

"So you're thinking where?"

"Johns Hopkins is number one. Mom and I visited there in February. I liked the campus and the curriculum."

"She told me all about it. You also visited the University of Maryland and the University of Delaware."

Her father was trying to compute the cost of those schools. Since his daughter's birth, Gary had socked money away for her college education.

"Believe it or not, Lizzie, your mother and I don't agree on a lot, but on your college education, we agree you should go to wherever you want. We've been good at saving since you were little. We didn't go on a lot of big vacations; we didn't go out to eat a lot."

Once dressed, they walked together from Bay Village to the Boston Common and made their way to the State House on Beacon Street.

"Have a good time, honey."

"Thanks, Dad." She hugged him.

"I love you."

"Love you back."

Lizzie entered the building by the statue of General Joseph P. Hooker, a Massachusetts native and mediocre Civil War general.

~ * ~

West of Boston, Summer Atkins started her morning in a funk. She hadn't slept well, awakening at 4:30. She checked her phone for a few minutes before getting into the shower.

When she was finished, Summer searched the refrigerator for an English muffin and some margarine. She found those and a bottle of orange juice.

Her father joined her. "You're up early."

She muttered, "Couldn't sleep. This really sucks."

He chuckled. "Tell me how you really feel."

"I thought I'd have a nice relaxing summer, but no, I have to work."

"It builds character."

"Bullshit."

"I heard that," piped in her mother, arriving in the kitchen. "Nice table manners."

Mom stepped in and reviewed Summer's apparel. "That won't do. Put on either a skirt or a pair of slacks. Those ripped jeans are horrible. You're going to work, not to a party."

Summer frowned.

So, this is my summer? Holy shit!

Begrudgingly, she changed her attire. Upon final review of her parents, she waved and got into the car. Her music screeched in her ears as her dad drove her to the commuter rail station, parked, let her jump on the train into Boston's North Station. She slept the entire ride into Boston. Only the rustling of commuters leaving the train woke her.

Summer gathered her pack, slipped off the train, and headed for Charlestown.

~ * ~

Not far from Charlestown, Mitch Ledowski awoke at five, showered, and dressed. He ate quickly. Mitch loved the early summer mornings when his seaside town was slowly awakening. He took a thirty-minute walk around town. Stopping at Dunkin', he bought a black coffee and a *Boston Herald*. Once he finished drinking and reading, Mitch hit the bathroom one final time before his drive to the Navy Yard. As the crow flies, the distance was only a matter of a few miles, but he had to contend with the blizzard of traffic lights in Winthrop, East Boston, Chelsea, and Charlestown. He listened to Frank Sinatra as he navigated. Once at the yard, he parked and headed to the destroyer, which he felt was his second home. He hailed several sailors over at the *Constitution*. He was about to step onto the gangplank when Benny Goodman walked up.

"Hello, Mitch. I have two interns, a boy and a girl. Would you mind giving them the grand tour?"

"Mr. Goodman, it would be my pleasure."

"I'll send them over about ten o'clock."

"Aye, aye, sir," answered Mitch with a wave.

Benny smiled and waved back.

I hope I'm that happy when I'm his age.

Fifteen

Arrival: Navy Yard

To his right, Gordon Beckwith saw the *U.S.S Constitution* and the *U.S.S. Cassin Young*. He didn't think he'd ever want to sail on either ship or ever join the Navy.

An old man with a navy-blue baseball cap with the U.S.S. *Cassin Young* inscribed in white in the front waved to Gordon. "Hi, there, young fellow."

Gordon waved back. "Hi."

As he approached the museum, he heard someone behind him muttering, "I can't believe this. This really sucks."

He turned and saw a girl with a head of blond curls wearing a pink shirt and a denim skirt.

She looked up. "What're looking at?"

"I heard someone squawking behind me. I was curious."

"Are you a tourist?"

"Do I look like one?"

"Nah, you're probably a jock with a Boston Bruins backpack. Are you working here?"

"I think so. You?"

"Yeah, my old man is making me work this summer. I wanted to chill out at our place in Maine, but he ordered me to work."

"Oh." Gordon noticed she had a pretty face with two dimples and light green eyes.

"What's your deal?" she barked.

"My dad helped me get this job."

"Were you bummed about it?"

"No, because if I didn't work here, I'd probably be cleaning the bathrooms at his liquor store, lifting booze, and picking up trash in the parking lot."

"Ever sample some of the product?"

"No. I'm an athlete. Some guys have got caught drinking and were suspended from playing. I love to play. I wouldn't want to jeopardize that."

Summer rolled her eyes. "Ah, you take no chances."

"Not of those kinds."

They made it to the front door. In front of them was a gray, granite building, home of the *Constitution* Museum.

Summer whispered, "You don't smoke weed, do you?"

"Sorry, not interested."

"Jesus, you are Captain America."

Summer stomped toward the building. Gordon followed.

This isn't a great start, he thought. *I'm stuck with a stoner, even if she's gorgeous.*

Inside, they found Benny Goodman. He looked at the two new employees.

Why do we need interns? This is just babysitting. I wish we didn't have them.

The trustees thought interns may later turn into supporters and maybe future employees.

Benny's dense black hair was askew. He had slept poorly and was hungover.

He waved the teens into his office. "Sit."

He looked at both of them with bloodshot brown eyes. He spoke with no enthusiasm. "Summer Atkins and Gordon Beckwith. Welcome. I'll be handing you off in a moment."

His head started to pound. His breath tasted like last night's supper—foul and oily.

Did I brush my teeth? I can't remember.

There was a glass bowl of hard candies on his desk. He unwrapped two peppermints and popped them in his mouth. He offered none to the teenagers.

That's better. I have to find my toothbrush.

He opened a side drawer of his desk and found his work toothbrush and toothpaste. Benny exhaled slowly.

"You both come highly recommended by your teachers."

Goodman swept his hair from his forehead. He worried about thinning.

Do those hair transplants really work? They're probably expensive.

"If you don't love history, you shouldn't be here because this is all about the experience. We'll give you some information about the history of the Navy Yard, the *Constitution*, and the *Cassin Young*. You will retain some basic knowledge about the surroundings, especially if someone from Paris or Tokyo asks you a question."

He stood and plucked another candy from bowl, again not offering any to his interns.

Benny swished the mint and hit a few back molars. One felt chipped.

Shit, now do I have to worry about my teeth, too? Am I really going to seed?

He refocused. "You'll help out wherever we need you. You could be cleaning, moving stuff, and giving directions. Please be pleasant, please be cheerful. We are a non-profit foundation which relies on contributions. Whatever you do helps us."

He looked at them. "Questions?"

No one responded.

"Okay, I'll turn you over to Emma Wollensky, our director of programs."

He walked them next door to her office.

"Hello," she said with a smile. "Welcome to the *Constitution* Museum."

She waved them into chairs but remained standing.

Gordon was trying to guess the age of this tall and thin lady with short black hair. Twenties? Thirties?

She had clear skin, brown eyes that twinkled, and perfect teeth. Her dress was informal with a ripped pair of jeans and a crimson Harvard t-shirt.

"I don't always dress this way. I apologize. We're putting together an exhibit on the history of the ship with some of the pieces from the *Constitution*. It can get dirty."

She talked with her hands in motion and paced. "I love being here. It's a historian's delight. Hope you like history."

Gordon nodded. Summer kept her emotions at bay. She just wanted to leave. She wondered what her boyfriend Cyrus was doing today... probably getting high without her.

"You met Benny, the big boss. My job is to show you around here and the property. I'll give you your assignments."

She tapped the side of her head. "You need a tour of the ships. You can leave your stuff here. I'll walk you over, and you can meet one of the docents."

"Docents?' asked Gordon.

"Fancy word for tour guides. They know everything about their ships, from stem to stern."

The trio stepped into the summer sun. A warm breeze whipped the flags in front of the ships. Tourists had already queued up before both ships.

Emma said, "*Old Ironsides* is the oldest commissioned ship in the U.S. Navy."

"And undefeated," chipped in Gordon.

"Correct. We'll cut the line."

They stepped up the gangplank. "I'm going to have one of the sailors give you the tour."

They walked up the gangplank to the ship.

Gordon felt wobbly as he ascended.

When they reached the deck, they were greeted. "Welcome aboard, I'm Seaman First Class Hakeem Oglethorpe."

The sailor was dressed in historical garb. He looked six feet tall and was Black.

"Welcome to the oldest ship in the United States Navy and—"

Summer broke in, "Undefeated in battle." The sailor smiled.

Oglethorpe shook hands with the interns. "Have you been aboard *Old Ironsides*?"

"When I was younger," replied Gordon.

"Never," said Summer.

Their guide showed them the cannon; he took them below decks. He gave them details about what life had been like on this thirty-eight gun frigate, one of six authorized in 1797 during President John Adams' administration.

Gordon felt a buzzing in his ears and still felt unsteady.

"Captain America, are you okay?" asked Summer.

"I'm fine."

"You look a little pale."

Gordon thought he heard a faint sound in his ears. *Cannon fire?*

Seaman Oglethorpe said, "Even nowadays there are plenty of things to do on this ship."

"Did you ask to be assigned here?"

"Yes, Gordon. I come from Fort Myers, Florida. I love history, and I wanted to travel."

"Do you like Boston?"

"I love Italian food."

"You've come to the right place." Gordon pointed to the North End.

"Yes, I've gone there several times. You can't beat the pasta and the pizza."

Summer said nothing and didn't really examine anything. Gordon had shot photos with his phone.

I can't believe this guy. He's such a nerd.

After an hour on the frigate, the teens and the seaman walked over to the *U.S.S. Cassin Young.*

The sailor said, "This is Mitch Ledowski. He knows everything, and he actually served on this Fletcher destroyer."

"Hi, kids, I'm Mitch Ledowski. Come aboard." His smile revealed bright teeth.

Oglethorpe said, "I'll probably see you two around. Good luck."

Gordon and Summer thanked their guide.

He saluted them and returned to his duties.

Besides his *Cassin Young* cap, Mitch wore a blue polo jersey, a pair of tan chinos, and white New Balance sneakers. He had white hair and a tanned face and stood five-feet, six inches tall with no belly.

Gordon again was trying to guess his age. *Old, but how old?*

"You must be Gordon, and you must be Summer. Welcome aboard."

Although the ship was berthed, Gordon grew a little queasy. After he and Summer walked up the gangplank, Gordon's legs felt a little rubbery as if the ship were cruising the sea. His stomach turned queasy. There was a slight buzz in his ears again. *Gunfire?*

Mitch started his tour. "Look around, guys, at this place, the Boston Navy Yard. From 1800 to 1974 the yard was in operation. Thousands of ships and vessels stopped here for repairs and to return to the seas."

Mitch had more energy than their previous guide. Even with shaky legs, Gordon took more photos. Summer's boredom ratcheted. She couldn't stifle a yawn.

Mitch caught her. "Summer, you may find this place boring, but this national park provided jobs for folks in the region."

Summer wanted to be anywhere else, but she pretended to pay attention.

"Just in World War Two, more than six thousand vessels were repaired by a work force of fifty thousand employees."

Gordon was fascinated by this. The Navy Yard must have been packed with workers and sailors.

Mitch said, "Enough about the yard, let me talk about destroyers, especially this one."

No matter how many times Mitch gave this talk, it still excited him.

He sipped water before continuing. "We still have destroyers working in the U.S. Navy today. The *Cassin Young* is one of the one-hundred seventy-five Fletcher-class destroyers that were built. They were called tin cans because of the thin plate of armor to protect the ship. Bigger ships like battleships and cruisers offered more protection."

Mitch escorted them up to the bow of the ship. "She's 376 feet, six inches in length, carrying five five-inch guns, ten torpedoes, depth charges, and anti-aircraft guns."

Gordon asked, "When was she built?"

Summer thought to herself: *this kid is such a kiss-ass. Who cares how old this tub is?*

Mitch knew a bored student when he saw one. "Summer, the ship was named after Commander *Cassin Young*, who won the Medal of Honor during Pearl Harbor. You do know the significance of Pearl Harbor?"

"Yes, the day that will live in infamy."

"Very good. The ship was built by the Bethlehem Steel Company in San Pedro, California. She was commissioned in 1943. Cassin Young's widow was present at the ship's launching."

Summer nodded, stifling a yawn. "I didn't know that."

Mitch took them through the ship, touring the captain's quarters, the galley, the ward room, and the engine room.

"Did you ever come under fire?" asked Gordon.

"No, Korea was mainly a land war, so I didn't. I'm thankful I didn't have to go through what the guys in the Second World War had to suffer. In under two years, the ship fought in seven campaigns and suffered two kamikaze attacks off Okinawa."

After the tour, Gordon thanked their guide. "Come see me anytime," said Mitch.

As they walked back to the museum, Summer broke the quiet. "This place sucks. My whole summer is stuck in this stinky place."

"I think it's cool."

"You would. You're a nerd."

"I love history, and I'm sorry you don't."

"I can't believe my dad got me this job. I should be home or at the beach."

"I'm fine."

They found a sub shop in Charlestown. They ordered and ate in silence. Gordon pulled out his book, *Six Frigates* by Ian Toll.

"You're reading, nerdo?"

"You're sulking, so I'm reading."

"What's the stupid book about?"

"The creation of six ships commissioned by President John Adams. One of the six is the *Constitution*."

"Are you a good student?"

"I think so. You?"

"School's always been easy for me."

"So, you're not challenged in school? You take AP classes?"

"Yeah."

"They're easy?"

"For the most part. My dad says I have a photographic mind."

"That's a nice thing to have."

"What's your deal, Beckwith? Are you going to college?"

"Hope so. You, too?"

"Not sure where. My dad lost his job, so I don't know what the money situation is."

"You can get scholarships if you're an excellent student."

She twirled her fork around some lettuce in her salad. "I don't want to go to a fancy school and end up in six-figure debt. Plus, with my dad getting laid off, I'm not sure how much they can help me pay. I don't know if scholarships would cover everything. U-Mass Amherst might be fine for me."

Gordon closed his book. "U-Maine Orono, a great place for hockey. My folks went there, I toured there, and I could see myself there."

"You'll freeze your ass off."

"Probably. I play hockey."

"So, you wouldn't go to school in a warm climate."

Gordon laughed. "Not to play hockey."

"Are you any good?"

"I play varsity."

Summer finished her salad, and they headed back to work. They spent the afternoon moving boxes and cleaning counters.

At four o'clock, they said goodbye. Gordon hauled his backpack and headed on his walk to South Station. He crossed the bridge into the North End and made his way to the Rose Kennedy Greenway. When he reached Faneuil Hall on Congress Street, he heard someone call his name.

"Gordon, wait up!"

Jack Quincy hustled to catch him. "You walk fast. I should've taken the subway to Back Bay."

"How was your first day?"

"I'm tired. I cleaned machines, I moved machines. I helped patients. I don't mind telling you I'm gassed. Double sessions in football are easier."

Along the greenway that bisected Atlantic Avenue, the boys saw a carousel with plenty of riders, a water fountain that spritzed bathers, and a beer garden. To catch their train, they didn't have the luxury to gawk. Gordon smiled while Jack struggled to keep up.

They joined hundreds of other commuters cloistered inside South Station. They bought water at the newsstand, waited for the train, and boarded ten minutes later.

As soon as the train started to move, Jack conked out, and Gordon returned to his book. When the ride approached Tiot Depot, Gordon roused Jack from his slumber.

"You're home, Jack."

"I can't believe I slept the whole ride."

"See you tomorrow."

Both headed for home. Jack went to bed at nine o'clock, astounding his father and brother.

Sixteen

Arrival: Library

As Gordon reported to work in Charlestown, Victor arrived at his summer job. Inside the third floor of the Massachusetts State House, he entered the George Fingold Library... his head swiveled at the railings above him, the file cabinets, and the volume of books.

I don't think I'll find my kind of books here. Skinny wouldn't like it here either.

"Good morning," said a lady with an olive complexion and raven black hair. "Are you Victor?"

Victor thought his mother was good looking, but this lady was breathtaking. He paused for air. Finally, he exhaled, "Yes, I am."

She walked around from the counter and shook his hand. She had a good grip.

"I'm Claudia Gomes, the library director. It's nice to meet you."

"Same here."

"I'm so glad you'll be helping us this summer." She motioned for him to sit down. "Do you patronize your branch of the Boston Public Library?"

"Not really. I buy my books instead."

"What do you like to read?"

"Fantasy and horror."

"Stephen King? Clive Barker? Neil Gaiman"

Victor smiled. "Yes, to King. The other guys, no."

"Read *Weaveworld* by Barker and *Neverwhere* by Gaiman."

Victor whipped out his phone and typed the two titles into his phone. "Thanks. I like to read new people."

"I'm going to have Mr. Puckett, one of our librarians, be your immediate boss for the summer. I'll tell you there will be a lot of lifting and looking up patron requests, so you can wear jeans, a nice t-shirt or jersey, and sneakers. Okay?"

He nodded. His mother wouldn't believe him about his dress code.

"Come on back, and we'll get you started. If you have questions or a problem, my door is always open."

"Thanks."

Victor walked behind the counter to the rear out of sight from patrons. A man with a white beard and white hair approached.

"You must be Victor."

"Yes, sir."

Puckett laughed. "Just call me Henry."

His boss wore black-rimmed glasses with a strap in the back. Puckett was six feet with a beer belly. His clothes consisted of a wrinkled white shirt, black pants, black sneakers, and a black tie that drooped over his gut. He had pale, pitted skin, signs of acne when he was younger, and gray eyes. "Miss Gomes gave you a quick overview of what you'll do. Right?"

"Yes."

"She said you can work in comfortable clothes?"

"Yes."

"Good, because you'll be lugging and cleaning stuff. I'm getting too old to schlep around with piles of books. This is one of the great libraries in Massachusetts. A lot of requests from the folks who work here: the governor, the lieutenant-governor, senators, representatives, other executive staff, and the public. Folks come here to do research, some come to search the internet, some to read reels on the microfiche readers, and some are tourists. Miss Gomes insists the place should always look welcoming and immaculate."

Puckett looked at Victor. "Ready?"

"I guess so."

"Follow me."

As directed by Henry Puckett, Victor hauled piles of books from one place to another. Some of the tomes were dusty and musty. He sneezed a few times.

Puckett asked, "Do you have allergies?"

"I don't think so."

"If you get bothered, you want to take an antihistamine like Claritin or Allegra. We also have masks to cut down on the mustiness."

Victor had taken off his tie and wished he had worn short sleeves. He had worked up a sweat.

Puckett examined his trainee. "Did you bring a lunch?"

"I was in a hurry. I didn't think of it."

His boss smiled. "C'mon. Do you like subs?"

"Yeah, they're okay."

The two of them exited to the rear of the capitol into Beacon Hill. They stopped at a plaque on a stone wall. Puckett pointed to it. "Do you know anything of the Barbary Pirates?"

"Heard the name before."

"You've heard of the U.S. Marines."

"Sure."

Puckett started singing the first verse of the Marine Hymn ending with "to the shores of Tripoli."

He pointed to the plaque. "This guy, William Eaton, with eight Marines and a bunch of mercenaries, took Tripoli a long time ago."

Victor read the inscription: "In 1805 Consul Eaton led a handful of U.S. Marines and a small army of Egyptians across 500 miles of the Libyan Desert to attack the port of city of Derna from the land. The city fell and the grip of the Barbary Pirates on the Mediterranean was weakened."

"It's too bad that's not taught in school." Puckett resumed their walk to a sub shop two blocks down the street. The shop was tiny.

"Best subs. It's a little out of the way. You won't find tourists here."

Victor opted for a steak with cheese, Puckett a meatball. He paid the tab. They ate quietly.

After they tossed their trash, Puckett asked, "What did you think?"

"Excellent. Thank you for paying."

"My pleasure. I don't eat out all the time. It's too expensive. You might want to brown bag it."

"Okay."

The rest of the afternoon featured more lugging. Victor couldn't believe it when it was four o'clock.

Henry said, "Okay, kid, time for you to knock off. See you tomorrow."

Victor nodded and stepped out into the public area of the library. When he did, he almost bumped into a pretty girl with reddish-brown hair.

"Sorry," he said. Victor kept the door open for her.

"That's okay." She smiled. He looked into her blue eyes.

Victor walked down from Beacon Hill to the Brooke Courthouse and caught a ride home with his neighbor. At home, he grabbed a water from the refrigerator and chugged. He changed out of his work clothes and plopped on the couch.

Victoria came home an hour later and whipped up supper while Victor told her about his day.

After the meal, Victor returned to the TV and watched an old Boston Celtics basketball game. Afterwards, he doused his face, brushed his teeth, and collapsed into bed by ten.

Seventeen

Arrivals: Secretary of State

Abbie Fortune caught up with her mother in the front of South Station.

"It was nice you had company on the ride," said Claudia Gomes.

"Yes, it passed the time."

They walked on Summer Street into the retail district, known as Downtown Crossing, which turned into Winter Street ending up at Tremont Street by the Park Street T Station. They crossed over and walked up the path on Boston Common to the State House with its golden dome.

"Very impressive, isn't it?" asked her mother.

"Yes, I agree."

"It's a great place to work."

"Even better when your boyfriend works in the same building."

Claudia smirked and chuckled. "We're both busy."

"Do you eat lunch with him?"

"Once in a while, not often." Claudia sipped from a bottle of Poland Springs. "Are you uncomfortable with me dating?"

"No, I'm not. It does feel weird."

"Your dad has remarried, so it's not like I'm cheating on him. During your father's absence, guys asked me out. I was still married, so I turned them down."

"I know. It just feels weird. You're dating my boss."

They waited for the light to change and walked over Beacon Street to the entrance past the General Hooker statue. After clearing security, they found the elevator to the third floor. They stopped at the secretary of state office.

"Abbie, you can hang out here in the library if you want to wait for me. You get out an hour before me, or you can take the earlier train home."

"I'll play it by ear."

"Good luck."

"Thanks."

Claudia kissed her daughter and headed for the library.

Inside the secretary of state's office, Abbie asked office manager Patti Cumberland where she should go and was directed to Doc Ott's office.

"Welcome," said a middle-aged man with wild white hair. "You must be Abbie."

Abbie saw two boys, one Black, one white; and three girls, one Asian, one white, and one with a terrific tan.

Abbie looked twice.

That can't be. Can it? Gordon's girlfriend from last summer? Crap. I hoped she was gone.

Ott gave the group a quick summary of their duties. The boss, Mark Preston, showed up a little later. He looked at Abbie and winked.

The secretary of state welcomed them and told them the many duties of his office. "You learn more about civics than in any school of yours. Welcome aboard, and I hope it's a good summer for all of you."

He left. Patti Cumberland came in and told them about their hours, code of conduct, and how they would be paid.

Ott took the kids down to Doric Hall where they started a tour of the building. Abbie enjoyed the tour and realized it must have been difficult for Gordon to leave this job. Whatever he encountered downstairs must have discouraged him from returning. Throughout the tour Abbie noticed Gordon's old flame staring at her.

After the tour, Ott joined them in the cafeteria. The interns ordered sandwiches and drinks. He gave them an hour alone.

Abbie grabbed her tuna fish sandwich and ended up next to Lizzie Soares.

Lizzie said, "I saw Mark Preston wink at you. Do you know him?"

Abbie was about to bite into the bread. "He dates my mother."

"Really?"

"Yes."

"Who's your mother?"

"Claudia Gomes, director of the state library."

Lizzie gave herself a dope slap. "I couldn't figure out who you were. Now I do. You're Beckwith's ex."

"Guilty as charged." She sipped her milk. "And you were his summer ex."

"Guilty. How is he?"

"Good."

"Do you still hang out with him?"

"No, but I saw him on the train this morning with another classmate."

"We had texted a few times during the year. I had hoped he'd come back this year, but something went on in Room 55 last summer. He tell you that?"

"Yes." Abbie was getting goose pimples talking about it.

"There is something different about him. Do you feel the same way?"

"Not at first. He was a jerk, a clown in junior high."

"Really? He seemed like he was a Boy Scout."

"In seventh grade, Gordon was suspended for putting booze in a teacher's water bottle. The teacher got sick."

"I can't believe it."

"Did he like you then?"

"No, I squealed on him, and that's why he was suspended for three days."

Lizzie laughed. "That must've made you popular."

"I was very shy then."

"What happened to change your mind?"

"We got stuck on a group history project. He was smarter than he let on."

Lizzie finished her water bottle. "Why didn't you survive as a couple?"

"I think we were too busy."

"I know how that is."

"We sort of broke up freshmen year. I started going out with someone else, and he turned out to be a jerk."

Lizzie rolled up her trash and threw into a nearby barrel. "Hey, that happens. I've met a few jerks. Do you want to get back together?"

"Sometimes yes, sometimes no." Abbie sipped. "Did you miss Gordon during the school year?"

"I didn't go out with anyone this year. I went to prom, but it was just a friend. I'm trying to concentrate on getting into a good school."

"I agree."

"Where is Gordon working?"

"He's an intern at the Navy Yard in Charlestown."

"He'll love that. We should go visit him."

Abbie nodded. "I'd be up for that. It would be a shock to him to see the two of us."

"Well, Abbie, this could be a good summer."

"I hope so."

For the remainder of the afternoon, Abbie ran around the building dropping off bills and mail to the various offices of representatives and senators. At four o'clock, she strolled from the secretary of state's office to the state library. She was almost run over by the handsome guy with blue eyes. He apologized and kept the door open for her.

Abbie pulled out her book, *Little Fires Everywhere* by Celeste Ng. She sat and read until her mother showed up at five o'clock. The pair walked to South Station and waited for their train.

They stood outside near the train track, Claudia still checking her phone for any emails and texts.

Abbie edged toward her. "You're never going to believe who I'm working with."

Claudia took a second and divert herself from the phone. "Who?"

"Gordon's last summer's girlfriend."

"Was it weird?"

"No, she was really nice. I liked her."

"That's nice. I have an intern, a boy your age. His name is Victor Santos. He likes fantasy and horror books."

"I think I bumped into him."

"You'll have to introduce yourself next time you see him.

Eighteen

Summer Sticks It Out

For the second day on the job, Summer Atkins was taking no chances. She stuffed a few joints in her purse. She needed something to help her cope. His first day did nothing for her. She wanted to quit.

She shared breakfast with her dad.

"Dad, I hate it," she said.

"Stick it out," said her dad. "First days can be a pain in the ass in any job. You feel awkward; you feel stupid. You don't know anyone, and they don't know you as a worker and as a person."

"The big boss was a dick. His underling was nicer."

"Anybody your age working there?"

"I've got this strait-laced jock who reads books. He's a big nerd."

Her father chuckled. "A jock who's a nerd. That's a new one on me."

"Can't I enjoy the summer without working?"

Dad grinned.

Summer spooned a few Wheaties. "Are we selling Maine?"

"I might have to."

"That would really suck." She frowned. "Where are you going to today?"

"Check out a few prospects. Unlike yourself, I like working, using my brain."

"On this job, you don't use your brain. You're a mule."

"Summer, you're a teenager, an intelligent teenager who smokes too much weed. You're not going to be the boss. Like all of us before you, you do what you have to do. I agree a lot of the jobs are labor intensive. There's no getting around it. You have to hump and lump it."

"Thanks. Just what I wanted to hear. Way to give me a pep talk."

"Honey, I'm not going to sugar coat it. You try to make the best of any situation. Hopefully, along the way, you enjoy certain jobs and work with some good people. Sometimes your co-workers can alleviate some of the drudgery. Some of my favorite jobs as a kid were because I liked the people I worked with."

"Where's Mom?' she asked before leaving.

"She isn't feeling well."

"Has she gone to work?"

"She called in sick," answered her father. "Losing my job has sent her over the edge."

"She's been taking her meds. Right?" Her mother suffered from depression.

"Yes, she's just in a dark place."

Melody Atkins had graduated from Salem State with a degree in elementary education and art. Summer missed when her mother would take her on trips to the Museum of Fine Arts or to the Isabella Stewart Gardner Museum. They both wanted to tour art museums in New York City.

Summer's frown remained in place. She finished her cereal, grabbed her bag, and headed into Boston.

She stepped off the commuter train at North Station, which was connected to the T.D. Bank Garden, home of the Boston Bruins and the Boston Celtics. Sports were lost on her. She walked by a statue of some stupid hockey guy flying through the air.

What's the attraction to sports? Who wants to go see some stupid game? I don't get it.

On Causeway Street, she lit a joint and made her way to the North Washington Street Bridge. By the time she crossed the bridge to Charlestown, Summer had steadied herself for her day at work. She fanned away invisible smoke.

Gordon Beckwith moved boxes and swept the floor. Neither he nor Summer saw Benny Goodman, but spent a good part of the day with Emma Wollensky.

"Are we going to lunch, nerdo?" Summer asked.

"If you want to. Same place?"

"I just want a salad. I'll be better company."

They walked a few blocks to the same sub shop.

Who walked in but Jack Quincy.

"Gordon!"

"Hey, Jack. This is my co-worker, Summer Atkins."

Jack thought to himself: some guys have all the luck.

"The pleasure is mine." Jack bowed.

Summer gave him a big smile. They ordered and took a table near the window.

She looked at the two guys. "Don't tell me, Jack. You're a jock."

Jack smiled. "Guilty."

"It's not table tennis."

"Football."

"Why are you here in Boston?"

"Working at the physical therapy place down the street. My dad's a physical therapist and got me the job."

"Do you like it?"

"I'm just a kid who's good at hauling stuff and cleaning."

She smiled. "Gordon's good at that, too. Are you a book guy like him?"

"Not guilty. I'd rather play video games. What about you?"

"I'm not a book junkie, and I don't do video games. My boyfriend and I play Magic, D&D, and a few other fantasy games."

"No Monopoly?"

"When I was a kid."

Food came and was devoured quickly. Jack finished first and headed off.

Summer and Gordon sauntered back to the museum. "He seems like a nice guy." Gordon nodded. "A good friend?"

"I've seen more of him in the last two days than the first two years of high school. We weren't friendly in middle school."

Summer pulled out a joint and lit up. "Summer, do that away from me. I'll smell like crap when we get back."

"Doesn't bother me."

"Bothers me."

Gordon skipped ahead of her.

He kept shaking his head. *She is one strange girl.*

Nineteen

Inbound to Boston

During the first week of work, Gordon, Jack, and Abbie met for the morning train ride into the Hub. Jack usually nodded off while the other two read. This Friday, Jack sat on the end seat with Abbie in the middle and Gordon by the window.

"Abbie," said Jack. She put down her biography of Isabella Stewart Gardner. "Gordon's at it again."

"What do you mean, Jack?"

"He's got another babe after him."

Gordon disliked interruptions when he was buried in a book. "What?"

"You should see this lady," said Jack. "She's blonde with curly hair and dimples."

Abbie grinned. "Do tell, Jack. You've met her?"

"We've gone to lunch a few times."

"Do you like her?"

"What's not to like?" added Jack. "She's sassy."

Gordon shook his head. "Jack's not telling you everything, Abbie. She's a stoner. She calls me Captain America because I don't smoke or drink."

Jack laughed. "At least not during soccer or hockey season."

"Jack, I'm not going to jeopardize my playing. Too many guys, and a few girls, have been suspended from sports because they got caught smoking or drinking. Hurt their teams as well."

"You are Captain America, Gordon."

"It's who I am."

"You've never tried anything?"

"Nope, but Abbie converted me to tea."

Jack chuckled. "Wow, that's exciting. You're a tea addict." He turned to Abbie. "Same for you?" She nodded.

Gordon closed *Six Frigates*. "Okay, Jack. Are you still a big-party guy?"

"I got hammered with Buddy LaFleur a couple times last summer. I came home sick. Dad was bullshit and grounded me for a week. I've stayed away from the party scene this year."

Abbie said, "I'll stick to my tea."

Jack said, "Never tried it."

"Very soothing, Jack. There are many kinds."

"Tea soothes you, Gordon?" Jack wanted to laugh.

"I just like the taste. Just a little milk and sugar will do it."

Abbie tried to suppress a smile. Jack and Gordon stared at her.

"What is it?" asked Gordon.

"Well, since we're talking about Gordon and the ladies, I have something to add."

Jack said, "Aren't you one of Gordon's ladies, too?"

Abbie blushed. "Yes, Jack, I was. I was the first of Gordon's ladies. Should I tell them about Number Two?

She sat in silence for a minute. "Guess who I've run into at the State House?"

Gordon felt funny. He knew the answer. "Lizzie Soares."

"Yup, she's back again this summer."

"Who's she?" This was from Jack.

"Gordon's crush from last summer."

"Is she hot?"

"Tall, athletic, black hair, tanned. Definitely hot."

"What happened?" Jack looked at Gordon.

"Geography," replied Gordon.

"What?"

"She lives in Plymouth. I don't have my license yet. It wasn't going to work."

Abbie said, "She has hers."

Gordon had really tried to keep grades and sports in the forefront of his mind, but the thoughts of Lizzie Soares reappeared from time to time.

"So, you two now know each other?" asked Gordon.

"Sort of. I like her."

Jack just laughed. "Gordon, I love all this drama. Why can't I be this lucky?"

"No girls in your life, Jack?" Abbie asked.

"Not at the present."

"I'll keep an eye out for you."

"I'd appreciate any help." He put his hands out. "But I'm not desperate."

Abbie grinned. "Got it."

Gordon laughed. "Only Moose is."

Twenty

Uncharted Territory

Abbie liked to explore downtown Boston. She liked history, but not as much as Gordon. She just enjoyed the hustle and bustle of the city, starting from the commuting experience to stepping out at lunch. Abbie strolled down Beacon Street along the Boston Common crossing Charles Street to the Boston Public Garden. She took her lunch, sat on a bench, read a book, or watched the people. She was tempted to ride on the swan boats in the lagoon, but she thought it might be weird riding by herself.

She liked her job at the secretary of state's office. She felt like she was tracing Gordon's steps within the State House. Her immediate boss, Doc Ott, was a good guy, and she liked her co-workers, even Lizzie Soares. They tried to avoid any more conversation about a certain male hockey player.

Did Gordon like Lizzie more than me? Did he really not want to go out with me this year because of studying and sports, or was that an excuse? Looking back, he was right. Although I enjoyed being single, I missed Gordon. We shared a few classes, but I would've loved to see him on a weekend.

In the midst of this self-examination, Abbie's thoughts were interrupted by a visitor.

"I know someone who liked to come here," said Lizzie Soares, who carried a blue Plymouth North water bottle.

Abbie looked at her. "Do I get one guess?"

"Can I join you?"

"Sure."

"Abbie, he even dragged me onto the swan boat." She chuckled. "I even liked it. Maybe it was the combination of the weather, the scenery, and him."

"I could see that. I was just thinking back to the past year. We agreed not to hang out."

"How was it?"

"It was okay. I missed him."

"Did he see anybody else?"

"I think I would've heard. Girls always talked about him."

"What about you?"

"No. Did you see anyone?"

"I asked a friend to take me to the junior prom, but that was it."

Lizzie swigged water; Abbie chewed an energy bar.

Lizzie said, "How's his new job?"

"He doesn't say much about it on the train, but our other rider, Jack Quincy, says there's a hot blonde who works with Gordon at the museum."

"Did Gordon say anything about her? "

"No, he just said, 'She's a stoner.' Jack likes her.'"

Abbie crumpled her lunch bag, stood, and tossed it into a nearby trash barrel. Lizzie followed her.

"Lizzie, there's someone who I might be interested in. Victor Santos works for my mother in the library. He lives in the city."

"Why don't you ask him out?"

"I don't think I could do that. Plus, it's a matter of geography."

"Gordon and I didn't let that bother us."

Abbie nodded. "You're right. I have my learner's, but I need my dad to take me out to drive. I don't know Victor's situation. I'd rather he make the first move. I don't want to be rejected."

Lizzie shoved her lightly. "A guy would be crazy to turn you down, Abbie."

Lizzie grinned. "Maybe this Victor is worried about asking you out because his boss is your mother."

"I never thought about that."

"A first move by you might put him at ease."

"Thanks, Lizzie. We should head back."

As they stepped out of the public garden by the Make Way for Ducklings statues, Lizzie said, "This is going to sound crazy, but I'd still like to see Gordon. Not to go out or anything, but just see him and talk. He's a good guy."

"Lizzie, I see him every day on the train. Maybe we can walk down to the Navy Yard either at lunch or after work and surprise him."

Lizzie almost choked on her water. "That would be quite a surprise. Imagine him seeing the two of us together?"

Abbie nodded. "It would be fun to see how he would react to that sight."

The light turned green on Charles Street, and they crossed over to the Boston Common, and back to work.

Twenty-one

Library Worries

Victor Santos was worried. Should he ask out Miss Gomes' daughter? What if Abbie turned him down? Would his boss be unhappy with him dating her child?

Besides those concerns, he enjoyed working at the State House library. He liked the big boss, Claudia Gomes, and his supervisor, Henry Puckett.

His neighbor Gus drove him to and from work, so Victor caught a break not having to ride on the MBTA. Today, Gus and Victor left Mattapan enroute to downtown. The two of them mostly talked about the New England Patriots and the Boston Celtics.

Gus reminded his passenger, "I was a pretty good ballplayer at English High School. I was the center on the football team and center on the basketball team."

Victor asked, "Did you play in college?"

"I was a fool in high school and ignored the books—not the ladies. I barely graduated, so I joined the Navy. I smartened up later and got my degree when I was older. Who knows, I might've gotten a scholarship to a small college, but I was bored in the classroom. Education matters. How are your grades?"

"Okay, Bs and Cs."

"Room for improvement?"

Victor laughed. "You sound like my mother and one of my teachers."

"Well..."

"Yeah, probably."

Gus turned his car right onto Beacon Street. "If you get good grades, it will help get into a college of your choice."

"I'd have to go a state school. Maybe commute to Bunker Hill Community College for two years and go somewhere else to finish."

Gus stopped at the red light in front of the State House and by the memorial to the 54th Infantry Regiment.

"Victor, you can do it. Don't be a dope like I was. It took the Navy to smarten me up."

"Thanks, Mr. Saunders." He hopped out.

Victor entered the building by the Hooker statue. After he cleared security, he headed for the elevators.

"Victor, wait up," hailed a voice.

Abbie Fortune hustled to meet him. He smiled. "Hi."

"These elevators can be tricky. I could be waiting for ages."

Victor caught a whiff of her perfume through her auburn hair and noticed the light shower of freckles on her neck. They got off on the third floor. Walking down the hall, he was entranced by her.

She stopped at the secretary of state's office. "I'll see you later this afternoon."

He grinned and nodded.

Why didn't I say anything? What happened to my voice? I should've asked her what she was doing for lunch. What would Skinny do in my place? Would he have a slick line?

Victor signed in at the main desk and walked into the back. He put down his backpack.

Henry Puckett, wearing his usual long-sleeve white shirt and black tie, saw Victor walk in.

"Victor, are you okay?"

"Henry, can I ask you something? You're an old guy."

"I hope I'm not too old at forty-five. It's the white hair and the belly that does it."

"I came in with Abbie Fortune, and I didn't say anything. I was tongue-tied. That ever happen to you with girls?"

"Victor, it's probably the reason I'm a bachelor. I would try to ask someone out, and I was paralyzed with fear. I felt like I was going to either throw up or go the bathroom. It's not unusual to freeze up with the ladies with some guys. I was one of them."

"I'm also afraid because she's Ms. Gomes' daughter. Would she be mad at me?"

"Miss Gomes is a fair boss. She may be protective with her only daughter." Henry took off his glasses and rubbed a lens with his thumb. "What the hell. Give it a shot. That way you'll know. If you don't, you'll regret it later."

"I was worried Abbie would say no. She probably has a boyfriend. Then I was worried about what her mother would say."

Henry said, "You won't be kicking yourself if you don't try."

The rest of the afternoon flew by for Victor. He crated books and cleaned up the backroom.

Twenty-two

Jitters

By the end of the work day, Abbie was tired after running around the capitol. She made it to the library at 4:05 p.m. Lizzie Soares winked at her as she headed down the hall.

Abbie said hi to her mother and Henry Puckett at the front desk. She had a book in her backpack, but she felt like she couldn't concentrate, so she stared out overlooking Beacon Hill. She checked her phone, but nothing of note popped up on the screen.

At four-thirty, Victor Santos appeared from the back room. He saw Abbie and waved. Abbie stood and waved Victor into the hallway. He followed.

"How're doing, Victor?" she asked, nervously.

"Good, Abbie."

She looked into his blue eyes. "I've never done this before."

"What's that?"

"Asked a guy out."

"Really?"

"Really."

He smiled. "You're asking me out?"

"Yes, because I figured you were too shy because of my mother. Am I correct?"

"Yes."

"I don't have my license."

"Neither do I."

"What about tomorrow?"

"I was going to hang out with my buddy, Skinny, but he'd understand."

Abbie knew her mother would be closing the library in a minute. "I've got it. Do you know Legacy Place in Dedham?"

"Yeah, my mother and me have gone shopping there."

"The commuter rail stops right by it. We can meet at J.P. Licks."

Abbie grabbed her phone. "Victor, check out the Saturday schedule on the MBTA."

He took out his phone and reviewed the schedule. They looked at the times and agreed to meet at 3 p.m. They typed each other's numbers into their phones.

Abbie caught the glimpse of her mother heading toward them. "See you tomorrow?"

"Sure. Looking forward to it."

Victor scooted away to catch his ride.

Claudia had seen the two teens talking in the hall.

She smiled. "You two making plans?"

Abbie blushed. "Mom, really?"

"I'm not surprised. Victor is a nice boy. What're you doing?"

Abbie told her. On the train ride home, Abbie texted Lizzie with the news. She replied with a thumbs-up emoji.

Lizzie kept thinking about Gordon Beckwith as she walked to her father's condo in the South End. She had hung out a few times with a few different guys but romance never blossomed from those encounters. Still, she enjoyed the rare texts from Gordon over the course of the school year.

She wondered if he had changed in his appearance. He had wanted to add some height and some muscle to his frame.

I don't think Abbie would mind if I saw him. She thought Victor Santos was good looking.

~ * ~

Abbie's new interest waited for his ride, still shocked by her proposal. Court officer Gus Saunders picked up Victor in front of the courthouse. He jumped into the SUV.

Gus asked, "How was your day?"

"Pretty good. How was yours?"

"A prisoner crapped his pants, a juror had a diabetic seizure, and I didn't have my lunch. Other than that, it was just another day at the ranch."

He turned to his passenger who almost smiled. "What's really up?"

"A girl asked me out."

"No way?" Gus laughed. "I wish a girl would ask me out. Of course, I'm old."

Victor said, "What was funny was I was going to ask her out, but her mom is my boss."

"That could be tricky. So, what're you two going to do?"

Victor gave Gus the plan.

"Tough without a license, but you'll make do."

By the time Gus entered Dorchester, he stopped at a red light on Morrissey Boulevard.

"Tell you what. I'll give you a ride to Dedham, and you can take the train back into town. Also, I'm starving. Is your mom expecting you for supper?"

"She won't be home until later because of her shift."

"Let's grab something to eat. What do you say?"

"Sure."

"And you can tell all about your mystery lady."

Twenty-three

Ice Cream & Bowling

While Gordon was cleaning the bathroom of his father's liquor store on a warm Saturday, his ex-girlfriend Abbie was stepping out for a date. Abbie had crept back into his thoughts recently. He loved seeing her on the commuter train, but, besides that, he missed spending quality time with her. Gordon also wondered about Lizzie Soares. He got the impression that she and Abbie had hit it off at their summer job. Abbie had mentioned her a few times in conversation, but the topic of Gordon between the two girls was not relayed to him. He missed Lizzie, too, but the two of them going out had occurred a year ago. Summer Atkins seemed friendlier to him. She had stopped smoking and complaining about her life. She hinted about hanging out outside of work. Like Lizzie, there was the issue of transportation. Since Gordon only had his learner's permit, Summer told him she'd drive to Tiot. His other issue was helping his dad at the store on the weekends.

He said his father unfortunately needed him this weekend at the store and help at the parking lot with a few upcoming concerts at Gillette Stadium.

~ * ~

As she prepared for her date, Abbie wasn't thinking of Gordon. Her mother offered to give her a ride to the shopping area in Dedham, but Claudia told Abbie she would have to take the train back home since she had a date with Mark Preston.

"Two dates for us, Abbie," said Claudia. "It's been a long time for you."

"Yes, it has," Abbie said, trying to brush away split ends from her chestnut hair. "I have crappy hair, not dark, straight, and lustrous like yours."

"You have lovely color."

"Maybe, but it can be unmanageable. I got Dad's hair."

"Have you heard from him, the new dad?"

"Just a few texts."

"Have you seen the baby?"

"Just on my phone. I would like to meet my baby brother."

"Give him some time. Things are crazy with an infant."

"Are you mad or sad?"

"No, I'm happy for him. Your father seems like he's in a good place."

"Did you wish you'd had more than one child?"

"I do, honey. We tried. Then he took off."

Abbie gave up trying to tame her hair.

Claudia checked out her daughter. "You look pretty."

"I hope so."

~ * ~

As they drove to the destination, Victor Santos rode to his in Gus Saunders' car. They pulled into Legacy Place and turned past L.L. Bean.

Gus pointed to the right. "I see J.P. Licks." Victor nodded. He was so nervous he hadn't eaten lunch. Gus curled into a parking space opposite the ice cream store.

"Victor, you've got this. Be a gentleman. Always allow the lady to enter first. Be yourself and have fun."

"I hope I can move my tongue."

"You'll be fine." Gus put his fist out to Victor who opened for a handshake. When they shook, Gus palmed off two twenty-dollar bills.

Victor was shocked. "Gus, thanks. I've got money. I owe *you*."

"No, you don't. Just have a good time. I want a full report on Monday."

Victor slipped out the passenger door and waved as Gus pulled away. He stood next to a bench by J.P. Licks. He and Abbie had agreed to meet there at three o'clock. Victor checked his watch. The time was 2:55.

He didn't wait long until a blue Subaru SUV stopped next to him. He recognized the driver as his boss, Claudia Gomes. Abbie got out of the car; her mom drove off.

Victor looked at Abbie who wore a blue jersey, pink shorts, and pink sneakers. He wore black shorts and a white collared jersey. That morning Victor had remembered to shave and use cologne.

"Hey," he said.

She smiled. "Hey, you."

He turned and looked at the ice cream shop. "Would you like one?"

"Sure."

They walked inside, ordered their flavors, and ate them outside on a bench. Victor kept his eyes on Abbie. He paid so much attention to her, his ice cream started to drip. If someone asked him at that moment about the weather, Victor couldn't tell if it was sunny or snowing. The weather didn't matter.

After they finished, Abbie asked, "Do you like working at the library?"

"Yeah, it's good to have a paycheck. I can help out my mom."

"I agree."

"Do you come to work with your mom?" Victor's nerves finally settled.

"Yes, but in the morning, I sit on the train with two friends from school. She lets us alone. And you know, I wait and take the train home with her."

"How's your school?" she asked.

"Catholic high school... old, but it's safe. I take the T to school. You?"

"Public, a decent size. I like it."

"You're a good student. Aren't you?"

"I've always liked school. I grew up in the town library. It was my comfort zone."

"What does your dad do?"

"My folks are divorced. Dad sells cars. He got remarried and now has a baby boy, my half-brother."

She explained Jack Fortune's ill-fortune with gambling, his disappearance for five years working to pay off his debts, and his unsuccessful reunion with his wife.

Victor's blue eyes widened. "That's wild. You thought he was dead?"

"Yes. I missed him big time. What about you?"

"Never met my father. I don't know who he is. Mom won't tell me. I don't know if he's alive or dead. Mom's not sure either."

"That sucks."

"Big time. If he's alive and I met him, I don't know what I'd say to him. 'Thanks for nothing.' Thank God my mother didn't abort me."

The conversation was hitting dark spots for Victor, so he switched the topic. "You like bowling?"

"Sure."

"Let's go."

Abbie had only bowled with smaller candlepins and had never tried the big balls. Victor coached her. They played three strings. She was competitive.

Victor said, "You sure you're not a ringer? You've played before."

She laughed. "Only the smaller balls. We have an old bowling alley in Tiot."

After bowling, Victor found a place with hamburgers. Gus' donation helped out with the food, which was good.

After supper, Abbie took Victor's hand, and they strolled the stores. Abbie looked at her watch.

"I have to catch my train."

The two teens walked behind the shopping center and through an apartment complex to the train station. They waited for five minutes until the engine approached.

"Victor, this was great. Thank you for a nice day."

She kissed him on the lips. "Do it again soon?"

"Absolutely." He smiled.

When the train stopped, Abbie was about to step into the car. She turned, flashed him a smile, and waved.

Victor waved back and watched the train pull away. He walked over to the other side to wait for his inbound train. On the way home, he didn't bother to look at his phone. He couldn't wait to tell Gus on Monday.

Twenty-four

A Beautiful Sunday

Ever since he woke up, Gordon felt something was going to happen. He wasn't sure what would occur, but the morning appeared in dark light. This Monday in July shuttered sunshine and opened its window to dark clouds, making it an unusual summer's day with a cool breeze. When Gordon and Jack walked over the North Washington Street Bridge to Charlestown, both wished they had worn a light jacket to ward off the chill from the water.

"Jesus, it's freezing, Gordon," said Jack. "This can't be July. Feels like October, and I have to suit up for a football game. I wouldn't mind this kind of day during double sessions next month."

"It's New England, Jack," answered Gordon. "I should've brought my skates. I feel like I have a hockey practice."

They split to their separate destinations. Later that day at lunch, Gordon went to look for Mitch Ledowski on the *U.S.S.*

Cassin Young, DD-793. Gordon wanted to ask Mitch about teaching, and if that was the career he should seek.

He stepped onto the visitor entrance near the rear of the ship. Mitch was nowhere to be seen. Gordon had begged off lunch with Summer and Jack. He told them he wanted to read his book and step away from the throng of tourists, which was hard to do in the peak of the summer pedestrian traffic.

As he headed for the destroyer, he swerved from all the visitors trying to get onto *Old Ironsides*. When he stepped onto the main deck of the ship, Gordon briefly lost his balance.

Must have landed funny on my left foot, he thought.

His equilibrium remained unsteady, and he walked through an open door midships. Mitch was nowhere to be seen. On the wall to the left was a photo of Captain Cassin Young. Gordon stopped and studied the picture of the man after whom the destroyer was named.

What was it like to have a ship named in your memory, he asked himself. It was probably the same for the people who had cities, buildings, and playing fields named after them.

Gordon tapped the tips of his fingers of his left hand on the picture. He swooned and blacked out for a moment.

When he regained his senses and his balance, Gordon was sitting on the deck of a ship, not the *Cassin Young*.

Where am I? It's not Charlestown? What kind of ship is this? It's kind of ugly. Holy crap, is that the U.S.S. Arizona *next to it?*

The cold and gray of the Boston Navy Yard was replaced by a soft, warm wind and bright, early morning sunshine. Then he noticed he sat in a harbor with many ships, U.S. Navy ships. There were palm trees. This wasn't Charlestown, Massachusetts.

Gordon grew nervous. He had a very bad feeling about where he was.

"Hey, sailor, are you okay?" asked a tall teenager in civilian clothes. "Did you drink too much last night?'

This young man with bright blue eyes stood over six feet in height with a golden crewcut. His short-sleeved shirt revealed muscular arms and large hands.

"I've never seen you on this ship. New?"

Gordon tried to sweep the fuzz from his brain. There was something familiar about this guy.

He can't be who I think he is. Can he?

"Seaman Buster McKinley from Bath, Maine, where we build ships, but not this tub."

Gordon shook his hand. "Gordon Beckwith, Tiot, Mass, just outside of Boston. What time is it?"

Buster checked his watch. "Almost seven-thirty. I was going to go to Mass. Were you?"

"I'm not Catholic," replied Gordon. "What's the date?"

Buster laughed. "You really must have had a rough night. It's December 7, 1941."

Gordon shivered. He knew it was a Sunday because the sailor was going to church. He knew the two of them were only minutes away from hell.

He pointed behind him to his left. "Is that the Arizona next to us?"

Buster laughed. "You are new. How could you miss that battleship?"

"Shit," said Gordon.

"What's the matter? Still hung over?"

"I don't drink. You're not going to make Mass." Gordon knew Admiral Isoruku Yamamoto's Japanese pilots were about to descend upon this peaceful setting and launch America into World War II. They would arrive in two waves for a total of 353 enemy planes.

"What're talking about? A launch always swings by for those sailors who go to church in town."

In the distance a drone of airplane engines thundered. "Those flyboys sure are loud."

"Buster, walk over to the starboard side. Quick!"

Gordon didn't want his grandfather to be killed by a Japanese plane.

"You're crazy What are you talking about?"

"Pearl Harbor is about to be attacked."

"Listen, friend, you definitely had too much to drink last night."

"Buster, I told you I don't drink."

With that, enemy planes swooped low into the harbor. Buster shook his head as he looked at the planes with the red circles under the wings.

"They're not American!" he yelled.

"Japanese!" replied Gordon.

"Holy shit! I'm trying to remember my battle station. I should be below up at the Bofors. Follow me."

Sailors, some in uniforms and others in civilian clothes, emerged from the parts of the ship. A man who might be the captain ordered Buster and Gordon to his side.

"You two hustle over here. Help me."

Buster whispered, "That's the captain."

The two teens flew to Cassin Young's side.

He turned to Buster. "Okay, seaman, let's see what his peashooter can do. How about some help."

Buster pointed to the ammunition, hefted some, and fed the gun. Standing behind the weapon, Captain Young fired at the planes with the red suns painted on their wings. Shells flew on the deck.

Gordon felt he could almost jump into a cockpit of one plane that was so close. He started to sweat.

I don't want to die before I'm even born.

Young trailed a plane and tried to time his line of fire ahead of a plane's path. No enemy planes dropped.

Explosions erupted everywhere. Geysers of water sprung up near the ship. Someone else fired back at the planes from the *Vestal*. A bomb struck the *Arizona's* magazine and rocked the *Vestal*. Captain Young, who had been firing, was tossed into the water. Gordon and Buster were knocked off their feet, but they stayed on the deck. Gordon's ears rang. Both boys checked for any injuries. There were none.

A sailor shouted, "The captain's in the water!"

Buster saw his commander bobbing in the oily water. He took off his shoes and dove into the dark water. Gordon wasn't confident in his swimming ability and hovered over the side of the ship. He watched Buster pull the captain to the surface and helped him swim to the ship. Captain Young coughed, his face blackened by oil.

Would the ship have to be abandoned?

The two swimmers made it to a ladder. Young climbed slowly with Buster behind him. When they reached the side, Gordon extended a hand. A powerful right hand clasped Gordon's forearm as Young stepped on board. Gordon helped Buster back on board.

"Thank you, seaman." Young coughed and wiped his blackened face. He turned around and shook Buster's hand.

"What's your name?" he asked.

"Seaman Buster McKinley."

"Seaman McKinley has just become First Seaman McKinley."

Buster smiled.

A few sailors were about to jump off the port side of the ship into black water. The *Vestal* had been hit by two bombs and had its power reduced.

Young shouted, "Get back here. You don't abandon ship on me!"

Young looked at the two of them. "I got to get up to the bridge and sail away from the *Arizona*."

The attack hadn't slowed. Buster looked at Gordon. "I gotta go, Beckwith."

Before he headed below, Buster asked, "How did you know there was an attack?"

"I had a feeling."

Buster scratched his head and ran away. Gordon didn't know what to do next. Despite its damage, the *Vestal* started to pull away from its berth toward safety away from the *Arizona*. Commander Cassin Young later earned the Congressional Medal of Honor for his exploits on December 7, 1941 and was promoted. Unfortunately, he was killed on his new ship, the *U.S.S. San Francisco* in late 1942 off Guadalcanal.

Gordon whispered, "*Vestal*."

With that, Gordon stood in the ward room of the *U.S.S. Cassin Young*. Despite the cool day, he dripped with sweat.

"Gordon, I didn't see you come aboard," said Mitch Ledowski. "I ran to get a coffee."

Gordon was dazed when he returned. His ears still throbbed. He couldn't believe he had stumbled into another portal to the past. The passage brought him to Pearl Harbor on "the day of infamy." On the following day, America had declared war on Japan. He had witnessed the horror and destruction of the event. Eighteen ships were sunk or damaged, 188 planes destroyed, and 2,403 sailors and soldiers died. Gordon had met the younger version of his maternal grandfather, just out of high school, slightly older than Gordon was. He also saw the bravery of Commander Cassin Young and his indomitable spirit to rally his ship and take it out of harm's way.

Mitch looked at Gordon's left forearm. "Looks like oil. You must've rubbed something on the ship, but she's fairly clean. Your shirt's wet, too."

Gordon said, "I have to run back to the museum. See ya."

Gordon flew off to the museum.

Mitch still was puzzled by the oil slick on Gordon's arm and the soggy shirt. Gordon slipped into the men's room and washed it off. A slight smudge remained.

He had met his grandfather and Cassin Young. Gordon's talk with Mitch about teaching would have to wait.

I thought my troubles were over, and they're not confined to tunnels.

Twenty-five

Ship Reflection

Gordon wordlessly completed his tasks after his visit to the U.S.S. *Cassin Young.*

Can this be happening again? This wasn't a tunnel like when I entered the past before when I was at the Tiot Library and at the State House.

He scratched his head and stopped for a moment.

Was the ship a tunnel to the past? How did I get back in time? It was the picture of Cassin Young. *I'll know now I better not touch it. I hope I don't have a problem if I step back onto the* U.S.S. Constitution.

Near the end of his shift, Gordon was bringing boxes into the museum's store. Summer tapped his shoulder.

"Nerdo, where are you?" she asked.

"Sorry." Gordon turned around to see Summer. "I'm sorry. What did you say?"

"Where have you been? You haven't been your usual effervescent self today. Jack was disappointed you didn't go to lunch."

"I'm just a little tired."

Summer grinned. "I thought you didn't like to party."

"I was home last night."

"No girlfriend?"

"I had one freshmen year, but I've been too busy."

"Wow, Gordon Beckwith, you are a nerd and a dud."

"If you say so."

Gordon returned to his task opening boxes with *Constitution* swag for tourists to buy.

Jack Quincy swung by the museum after work to join Gordon on their walk to South Station.

"You blew us off today," he said. Jack put out his hand and smiled. "I forgive you. I had the lovely Summer Atkins to myself."

"Good for you."

The cool, eerie start of the day had turned sunnier and warmer.

Gordon said, "For once, she didn't smell of weed. Too bad she's got a boyfriend and lives far away."

"You've got your license."

"Gordo, we only have one car. I don't think Dad would let me drive to the ends of the earth for a date."

Gordon chuckled. "Doesn't hurt to ask."

The boys had made it to the Rose Fitzgerald Greenway, a pedestrian walkway bisecting busy roads.

Jack sipped from his water bottle. "I think Summer has the hots for you."

"What?"

"I do. She kept asking me about you."

"Really?"

"She's hot."

"Agreed, but she's a GU."

"GU? What's that?"

"Geographically Undesirable. I had the same situation last summer."

Jack laughed. "I should have those problems with girls."

They walked to the entrance of South Station, which had been built in 1902.

Jack said, "It might be worth the ride to visit Summer Atkins."

"It might, but I only have my learner's permit."

Jack smiled. "Not for long."

On the train ride home, Gordon conked out while Jack picked up and read Gordon's book. Gordon dreamed of Hawaii in a different time.

Twenty-six

Mitch is Concerned

Benny Goodman was pissed off. He nursed a hangover for most of the morning. He had gone out last night for a quiet drink. One drink became too many drinks, and he paid the price for his consumption when he awoke.

Emma Wollensky had dropped off the monthly report for June. He looked at the figures and knew the trustees wouldn't be happy. Store revenues and museum donations had dropped recently.

He couldn't figure it out. June featured beautiful weather. There were various school groups visiting the *Constitution* and the *Cassin Young*, but the spreadsheet wasn't encouraging.

Are our exhibits too old? Do our surveys indicate approval of the exhibits? I think so. Don't we have great interactive features? Is the stock in the shop not appealing?

"I can't believe this," he said to Emma. He passed the report to her. Benny fished a peppermint out of his candy jar.

"Tough night, boss?" she asked.

"I should know better."

"You look horrible."

"Thank you. Why do you always look fresh as a daisy?"

She laughed. "Clean living. I work out, watch what I eat, and try to get enough sleep. You should try it sometime."

Benny ruffled his beard. "I did that years ago. I was a decent tennis player at one time, and I had a wife."

Emma laughed. "You could've fooled me."

"You can laugh. I was forty pounds lighter. Divorce changes a man."

Emma wondered if Benny had been born miserable. She hadn't seen much lightness emerging from his persona in her time at the museum.

She finished scanning his report. "We'll rebound this month and in August. We have new merchandise, and the park rangers have said attendance has recovered after last year's pandemic shutdown."

"Maybe. I get the impression my head's on the block."

"It's just nerves. You're young."

"This is my life. I need something to give us a shot in the arm."

"I'm proud of the museum," Emma replied. "Our surveys overwhelmingly approve of their visits."

"I know, I know. Just wish the numbers were better."

Emma left him to stew.

Mitch Ledowski dropped in before lunch.

"Hi, Mr. Goodman."

Benny waved his right hand without looking up from his computer. Finally, he swiveled toward his guest.

"Mitch, what brings my favorite docent to my office?"

"Mr. Goodman, have you noticed Gordon the intern recently?"

"I leave the interns to Emma. Has he done something wrong?"

"No, no. He's a good kid. Loves history."

"So why the concern?"

"He stopped over at the ship the other day at lunch and walked around the main deck."

"Did he steal anything?"

"No, no. I felt like he disappeared."

"Did he go below decks?"

"I don't think so. We've roped off access below decks because of Covid."

"I'm still lost about your concern."

"Benny, when Gordon reappeared, he looked haunted. And his clothes were wet, and his arm was stained with oil."

"He went swimming?"

"No."

"Could he have gotten wet on the main deck?"

"No."

Benny grabbed a mint out of his bowl and unwrapped it.

"Tell you what. I'll talk to Emma about the haunted kid."

"I just thought you should know. Gordon looked like he had seen a ghost."

"Thanks, Mitch."

Benny asked himself, is the destroyer haunted?

Mitch headed back to his post.

Benny scratched his head. A thought came to him. In his research about the Navy Yard, there had been talk of ghosts, but they were isolated. In the nineteenth century, someone working late in the rope walk claimed he had seen ghosts, images of sailors from the Navy Yard's past. Even in the twentieth century, a worker cleaning up in the commandant's house was spooked by an apparition.

Of course, ships have produced claims of specters aboard. Could there be ghosts here at the Navy Yard in the twenty-first century?

Could that be used in a promotional campaign? Why not?

For the first time in a long time, Benny Goodman grinned. He had forgotten about Mitch's concern about Gordon's destroyer visit.

Twenty-seven

Ghosts at the Yard

Benny sought out Emma, who was checking out the exhibition on the kinds of woods used in naval construction.

"Everything okay, Emma?" asked her boss.

"Fine, Benny," she replied, brushing black hair away from her eyes. "Somebody had run a pen across this piece of wood."

Benny bent down. "I don't see anything."

"I was able to wash it away. I like my wood to be pristine. It probably was a wise guy."

Benny looked around and checked out the visitors. He nodded his head toward the entrance.

He and Emma walked outside behind the railing by the dry dock.

She was puzzled. "What gives?"

"What's with that Beckwith kid?"

"Huh? What do you mean? Does he have a problem?"

"No, no. How do you find him?"

Emma laughed. "Gordon's been one of your best interns. He's a history nut. He just soaks up the place. He's a good worker. He asks good questions. I just wish Summer were a little more enthusiastic. I think she likes her weed, but I haven't smelled any in a while."

"Really? Should we fire her for smoking?"

"She's not incoherent. The first couple of days she was high, but Summer kept it under control."

Emma watched the visitors queuing up for *Old Ironsides*. "Why are you interested in Gordon?"

Benny pointed to the *Cassin Young* and related what Mitch had told him.

She frowned. "Maybe Gordon wasn't feeling well that day."

"How did he get wet?"

Emma thought Benny had been in good spirits today, especially since he had been in a funk recently. Maybe he was seeing someone instead of drinking himself into a stupor most nights.

Benny grinned. "Do you believe in ghosts?"

"I hadn't really thought about it."

"Do you?"

"I guess so."

"There have been accounts in the nineteenth century where sailors and civilian workers claimed the Navy Yard was haunted."

"Okay, I'm with you," she said. "Where are you going with this?"

"We promote a campaign of 'The Ghosts of the Navy Yard,' an exhibition and tour at the *Constitution* Museum."

"Hmm, not bad, boss. Also, we can promote it as a big event for Halloween. Wear your costume and visit the ships at the Navy Yard."

"Exactly."

Emma hadn't seen Benny this fired up in a while. She was still confused about the Gordon Beckwith questions.

She asked, "What's this to do with Gordon?"

Benny said, "When Mitch saw Gordon leave the ship, he looked as pale as a ghost. He wonders if Gordon saw a ghost during his visit."

"A ghost sighted on a ship during the day?"

"It can be dark in certain parts of the ship. That day was a murky and cold until late afternoon."

"I'll start putting down some thoughts for this promotional campaign."

"See that you do, Emma. It could do wonders for the museum. Improve fall attendance."

Emma chuckled to herself. And it works wonders for Benny's job security.

Twenty-eight

The New Chair

Clare Hopkins Fairchild had to fight her way out of the projects in Brighton, and she was used to getting her way.

Clare was the oldest of five girls, whose father had died early, leaving mother Bernadette to support the clan. She knew Clare was the complete package of beauty and brains. She constantly urged her daughter to succeed. Bernadette worked as office manager at the local Stop & Shop Supermarket. While Mom worked, Clare looked over her four siblings. Despite the drudgery, Clare loved her mother and didn't mind helping. Her only solace came from reading, usually just before going to bed.

Clare's burning desire was to escape the projects for a better life. She excelled in school and went on to graduate from Framingham State College with a degree in secondary education and a master's from U-Mass Boston. She taught mathematics in Boston schools and moved up the ladder to vice principal at Roxbury Latin High School. The principal was Harry Fairchild, a wealthy widower. Students caught wind of their romance, and she stepped away from teaching and launched a company that specialized in teaching math. They married and had a son, Jeremy, who had died in his teens a few years ago.

The chairman of the trustees had recently tendered his resignation after serving for many years. As a long-time donor to the *Constitution* Museum and a trustee, Clare felt the time was right to take over the reins for overseeing the place. The former chair, Winslow Mattingly, had held the position for many years. Since turning eighty, he decided to give up the ship, although Clare thought he had deserted it years ago. She envisioned a total revamping of the place and its approach to recruitment and donor solicitation. Her first target was Benny Goodman. She had met the director several times at various functions and was not impressed by him personally and professionally. She was impressed by his deputy. In his place, with the board's approval, she planned on appointing Emma Wollensky, who was younger, ambitious, and smart.

She decided to start making random visits of the museum and of the Navy Yard.

On a Monday morning, she drove her silver Mercedes SUV from her home in Lynnfield to Charlestown. She always enjoyed stepping onto the *Constitution* and the *Cassin Young*.

She parked and walked first to the *Old Ironsides*. She stood by the frigate in admiration, grinned, and moved over to the destroyer. After a few minutes of inspection of the vessel, she walked over to the museum.

Emma spotted the chairwoman and approached her.

"Welcome, Madame Chairwoman." They shook hands.

"Emma, it's Clare, no lofty titles."

"Nice to see you, Clare. What can we do for you?"

"Believe it or not, just consider me a tourist. I haven't visited the yard in a few months, and I wanted to check everything.

Pretend you didn't see me." She started to walk away. "Don't tell your boss I'm here."

Emma was surprised by the request, but she would honor it.

Why wouldn't Clare Fairchild want to meet the museum's director, Emma asked herself.

Emma couldn't remember Benny Goodman ever saying anything about Clare Fairchild. Benny and the former chair, Winslow Mattingly, were on good terms and had spent a few nights out together.

She thought Mattingly had given Benny a pass for the last several years, especially after Benny's divorce. He knew they had been drinking buddies.

What was Mrs. Fairchild up to?

Emma returned to her office.

Inside the museum, Fairchild walked up to the admission booth.

"How much to tour the museum?" she asked the volunteer.

"There is no set cost. We appreciate any kind of donation."

She smiled and dropped a hundred-dollar donation. The volunteer beamed.

Clare stopped at each exhibit. On the first floor, she saw a young man with blond hair pushing a dolly with boxes piled on it.

She caught her breath.

Oh, my. He looks like Jeremy, almost his double.

She tried to stop the welling of tears. She almost lost it.

Clare took several deep breaths and almost toppled.

"Are you okay, ma'am?" asked the dolly boy.

"Yes, I'm fine, young man. Thank you for asking. I just had a fright."

"Would you like some water?"

"That would be wonderful."

The boy parked the two-wheeler dolly. He put out his arm, and she leaned on him. He took her outside to a bench.

"I'll be right back."

He hustled inside, bought a bottle of water, and brought it to the woman in distress.

She took the bottle, put it next to her forehead, and then twisted off the cap. She sipped.

"Thank you, I needed that. What is your name, and what you do?"

"Gordon Beckwith, summer intern."

"How old are you?"

"Sixteen." *Same age as Jeremy was.*

"Do you like history, Gordon?"

"Love it. It's my favorite subject."

Gordon thought this woman was well dressed with a white pantsuit and pink sweater. Her hair was frosted; her skin showed only a few wrinkles. He couldn't guess at her age, but Gordon considered her attractive with brilliant teeth and deep blue eyes.

"What would you like to do when you get out of school?"

"Play pro hockey." He smiled. "Sounds like a dream. If not, teach history and coach hockey."

Jeremy had played hockey, and he loved history. Goose pimples spread across her back.

"It's good to have dreams. The world can use good teachers. Do you like to read?"

"Next to sports, it's my favorite thing to do."

"What are you reading now."

"I just started the Patrick O'Brian series. I had just seen the movie, *Master and Commander*, learned it was based on a novel."

She nodded. "It's a wonderful series. I believe the fourth book includes the *Constitution*. Mr. O'Brian visited the Navy Yard a few years ago."

She drank more water. "What about *Six Frigates*?"

"Already read it."

"Well, Gordon Beckwith, I'm so glad to make your acquaintance today. I hope I'll see you again this summer. My name is Clare Fairchild, and I'm the chairwoman of the museum's board of trustees."

She put out her hand, and they shook.

"It's been nice to meet you, Mrs. Fairchild."

"Same here."

She headed to her car.

Benny Goodman had just gotten up to look out his window when he saw the intern talking with his boss.

What's up with that?

He shouted, "Emma, come here!"

She ran into his office. He pointed out the window.

"Did you know Mrs. Fairchild was here?"

"I, I, just bumped into her."

"And you didn't tell me?"

"She wanted to be anonymous."

"Jesus, my second in command keeps a secret, and my intern is getting chummy with that woman. It's enough to drive a man to drink."

Emma suppressed a laugh. For Benny, it usually did.

"But I'm being good. I have my drinking under control."

"I hope so. I really hope so, especially with Mrs. Fairchild hanging around."

Twenty-nine

Eyes on Gordon

"Hi, Gordon," said Mitch as he hailed the intern the next morning.

"Hi, Mr. Ledowski."

Gordon couldn't believe someone like Mitch was so upbeat. He always had a smile on his face.

I hope I'm that happy when I'm that old.

"Are you doing okay?" asked the retiree. "Do you like the job?"

"Yes. I love coming to a place that brings history alive. The Navy Yard has the oldest commissioned vessel, and the U.S.S. *Cassin Young* of World War Two fame."

Mitch put a hand on Gordon's shoulder. "The reason I asked was that you looked upset when you stepped off the destroyer the other day. You looked like you had seen a ghost."

"Nah, I wasn't feeling great that day."

Is he physic? I did see a ghost, a lot of them.

"I came by to see you to talk about teaching. I couldn't find you."

Mitch couldn't remember where he had been that day, but he was distracted by a granddaughter who had been injured playing softball. "Okay, come by and see me again anytime at the ship."

"Sure." Gordon started to walk away and stopped. "Can I ask you a question, Mr. Ledowski?"

"Fire away."

"Are you always this happy?"

Mitch chuckled. "For the most part. My wife died a few years ago, and it threw me for a loop. I was mad at God for taking her away. I was miserable. My daughter kept trying to cheer me up. I just stewed. I was in a funk. She was the one who suggested I volunteer here. And, you know, she was right. I've been blessed with a great wife, great daughter, grandkids, and good health. Why be miserable? I'm thankful for every day. It's better to be above the grass than below it."

"Did you like teaching?"

"I taught history in Winthrop for thirty-eight years. I loved it."

"Who was worse... the students or their parents?"

"Gordon, because I lived in town, I knew a lot of the families. Most of the kids I had were good kids. Very rarely did I have a problem with the parents. Teaching has changed. They have to be recertified every couple of years. I was lucky. When I received my certification, it was for life. Also, the standardized testing doesn't allow a lot of teachers much leeway to tailor their lesson plans to their liking. It forces teachers to teach to the test and not necessarily to things they want to cover."

"I didn't realize that."

"It might be different if you teach in another state. Certification doesn't factor two things about teaching."

"What's that, Mr. Ledowski?"

"Obviously, teachers must possess the knowledge of the subject matter. Does a teacher like kids? And can a teacher communicate with students? Brilliant folks don't always make great teachers."

"It sounds challenging."

"It is, but it's rewarding if you can reach the students."

"Thanks for talking to me."

"Have a great day." Mitch smiled, waved, and headed back to the ship.

Summer Atkins pulled up beside Gordon. She turned toward Mitch. "He's a nice man."

"I agree." Gordon couldn't believe Summer had said something nice about anyone except maybe her boyfriend.

"You're not bad yourself, for a jock."

Gordon laughed. "What's up with you this morning? Are you already high?"

Summer said, "I stopped smoking weed. I don't need it."

"Wow, Summer, no recreational smoking."

"Don't make fun of me, Gordon. This has been a hard year. My father got laid off, and I don't think my parents get along. There's just a bad vibe in the house. I got high to escape, but my problems were still there. I had a pissy attitude. I did fine in school. Otherwise, I tuned out from a lot. I quit the ski team."

Gordon looked at her. "Your school has a ski team?"

"Yeah, it's no big deal."

"And people think hockey is expensive."

She punched him on the arm. "C'mon, we're expected."

Benny Goodman welcomed them just outside the entrance.

"Good morning, Summer. Good morning, Gordon."

The two teens looked at each other. "Emma's waiting for you guys," said the boss.

Summer whispered, "What's that all about? He usually barely acknowledges us."

"He looks neat. His beard's trimmed, his shirt is ironed, and he looks like he's had a haircut."

They met Emma, who assigned them their task for the morning.

As lunch approached, Summer said, "Do you want to go somewhere different for lunch?"

"I'm open."

"Let's go over to the North End for pizza. My dad told me I should try the original Regina's Pizza."

"Pizza's good for me. Want me to call Jack?"

"Sure."

Gordon pulled out his phone and dialed. After a few minutes of conversation, Gordon said, "Jack's tired. He said to go on without him."

"Okay, just the two of us, even better."

At noon they left the Navy Yard, walked over the North Washington Street Bridge, and stepped into the North End.

Gordon and Summer walked with no rush as they noticed tourists cluttering the sidewalks.

Gordon pointed to their left. "The *Constitution* was built just down the street."

"I know, Gordon. I do read the stuff in our building."

"I got carried away. We can go to the Old North Church afterwards."

She laughed. "We don't have time for a tour."

They crossed Causeway Street and strolled a few blocks to Regina's. They got a table and split a cheese pizza. Afterwards, they walked over to Hanover Street which bustled with cafés and restaurants and more tourists. Many folks ate outside. They stumbled onto Mike's Pastry, where Gordon bought each of them a cannoli.

"Gordon, I'm going to get fat." They sat outside at a table to enjoy their pastry when Summer almost dropped her cannoli.

"Oh, my God!" she shrieked. She pointed across the street. "My dad."

"Have him come over."

"No, no, he's holding hands with another woman."

"Hug me. I don't want him to see me." Summer nestled into Gordon's arms.

Gordon thought it was a good fit.

Summer peeked her head up. "He's gone. I can't believe it. Mom will be destroyed."

"Do you know the lady?"

"I'm pretty sure she was a co-worker."

"I'm sorry, Summer."

Gordon started to loosen his arms.

"I'm not sure how to handle this."

"Do you tell your mom?"

"Maybe I'll talk to Dad first."

Gordon checked his watch. "We should head back."

As they finished eating and got up, Summer grabbed his hand, and they walked back that way to Charlestown.

Thirty

Back to Bath

The next morning, Gordon was eating his Wheaties cereal when his mother came into the kitchen. Martha had just completed a treadmill workout. She wore a light blue U-Maine t-shirt with a matching pair of shorts. Her hair was pulled back into a ponytail.

She leaned and kissed her son on the cheek. "I'm a little sweaty."

"That's okay." Gordon drank some orange juice. "Mom, do you think we could visit Grandma again?"

"You'd like that?"

"I liked learning about your side of the family. I loved talking to Grandma."

Martha grabbed a paper towel and wiped her face. "I'm glad to hear you say that. She'd be thrilled."

She pulled out some diced fruit from a Pyrex bowl in the refrigerator and tossed it into a blender. When she was done, she poured the contents of her smoothie into a glass.

"Let me check with your father. If he doesn't need you this weekend, you and I can drive up Saturday morning and stay over for the night."

"That would be great."

~ * ~

Marty gave the two of them his blessing, and Martha and Gordon headed to Bath. Gordon drove the entire trip.

They grabbed lunch at the bakery they had visited the first time they went to Bath. Sure enough, the female barista hailed, "Hey, Mayor!"

"Hello, Kelsey, how's my favorite coffee maker?"

"Good, Mayor. I haven't seen you today."

"Just busy."

Curtis Bakewell surveyed the crowd. A young man and a woman were locked into their respective laptop computers by the window. He spotted a familiar face eating lunch with her son.

"Martha, what a pleasant surprise." He walked over to their table. "Good to see you, Gordon."

He shook Gordon's hand. "What brings you two back here?"

"Gordon wanted to see his grandmother, so we just came up for the weekend."

"Splendid. Please say hello to Agnes for me. Have a nice time."

The mayor grabbed his coffee and left.

Gordon finished his chicken salad sandwich. "He still likes you."

"Gordon, I'm married."

"It still doesn't mean he hasn't forgotten you. Has Dad ever met the mayor?"

"No, he hasn't, but he's heard a lot about him."

"From you?"

"Mostly from your grandmother. So much so that's why he hates coming here. Mom finally has let up as the years have gone by. Dad felt disrespected."

"She didn't make Dad feel he was worthy."

"No, but she had to accept that I love your dad and that's that."

Gordon smiled. "Otherwise, I might not be here."

They laughed.

At the McKinley homestead, they were welcomed by the matriarch. Agnes kissed them both.

"How wonderful for you to come to see me. We'll have a nice supper and play some Scrabble."

During supper, Agnes kept up a running commentary on the social and political affairs of Bath. After dessert, Martha and Gordon helped Agnes clean up.

Agnes asked, "Coffee or tea?"

"Tea, Grandma," replied Gordon.

"Gordon, you like tea?"

Martha said, "His old girlfriend turned him on to the wonders of tea."

"Old girlfriend as in ex-girlfriend?" asked Agnes.

"Yes, we agreed we had too much going on."

Agnes nodded. "Did you ever think of running for student council like your mother?"

"Not really. That doesn't appeal to me."

"What does?"

"Sports... hockey and soccer."

"Just like your grandfather. He was a good student. Although he didn't read books, Buster read newspapers and magazines."

"How old was he when he joined the Navy?"

"He signed up days before graduation, six months before Pearl Harbor. He was seventeen."

"Do you remember Pearl Harbor?"

"I was a young girl, but I'd never forget. It's one of those dates like JFK's assassination and nine-eleven that are indelibly etched upon your brain."

After dessert, Agnes brought out Scrabble. The players picked their first set of seven letter tiles. Scrabble went down to the wire, but Martha pulled it out over her mother and Gordon.

Agnes asked, "Do we need a redo?"

"Mom, I'm pooped," said Martha. "I'm going to call it night."

"Gordon?"

"I'd like to visit the study again."

"C'mon, let's go."

Agnes found a faded red photo album in a bottom drawer. "If he had a few beers, Buster would sit here, smoke cigarettes, and look at these pictures. I was always worried he would burn the house if he fell asleep while smoking." She frowned. "Him and his Lucky Strikes and his Ballantine Ale."

His grandmother opened the album and pointed to a grainy black and white picture. "That's his first ship, the *U.S.S. Vestal.* He called it 'an ugly tub.'"

"He was at Pearl Harbor. *The Vestal* was anchored next to the Arizona."

"You've done your homework."

"I love history. Dad's two fathers fought in Vietnam, nobody from World War Two."

She turned the page. There were two men in the photo in front of the *Vestal.*

Gordon pointed to them. "That's my grandfather and Captain Cassin Young."

"How did you know that?"

"Research. I work at the Navy Yard." Gordon didn't bother to tell his grandmother he had just met the two of them under trying circumstances.

"Oh, that's right." Agnes was touched by this interest of her grandson in her husband's naval career.

"Was Grandfather promoted after Pearl Harbor?"

"Why yes. How did you know that?"

Gordon coughed. "I think Mom mentioned it."

Agnes was really suspicious. Martha never bothered to ask her father about the war. "He only told me once he helped to rescue the captain when he was blown off the ship. After that he was promoted."

Gordon kept looking at the picture.

Agnes continued. "So, he didn't talk much about the war, but he spent a lot of time looking at these pictures. The other great irony of his service was that he transferred to his last ship, the U.S.S. *Cassin Young*, as you know, now permanently berthed at the Navy Yard. Before he died, we drove down there. Buster walked around the ship. He didn't say much. He showed what gun he worked on and other parts of the ship he worked on. We drove home in silence.

"When we were about to go to sleep that night, he turned to me and said, "Agnes, I love my country, and I loved my service, but there are some sights no one should ever see, especially a young man from Maine. Thank you for coming with me today."

Agnes' eyes moistened.

"He kissed my forehead and went to sleep."

Gordon turned a few more pages. "Gordon, I'm going to turn in. I wish you could've met your grandfather. Have you read all of his letters?"

"I've read a few. I'm pacing myself, tracing his voyages with the battles in the Pacific."

She kissed her grandson on the cheek.

"Good night, Gordon. Thank you for visiting me. God bless you."

"You, too, Grandma."

Gordon looked at the pictures of the *Vestal* and DD793, the *Cassin Young*'s ship number. He got up and opened the sea bag. He lifted his grandfather's work uniform which had been packed neatly. A sniff produced a touch of mold, so he placed it carefully back in its place.

When Gordon turned in, he wondered if he should tell his grandmother what had happened.

Not yet, he thought. *She'd probably think I was crazy.*

Thirty-one

Summer's Issues

Summer still had said nothing to her mother about seeing her father in the North End.

Melody had been busy with a few painting jobs, and her father supposedly had hunkered behind his computer looking for a job. Mom's job was paying the bills, and she was exhausted from working six days a week with long hours. Summer and her father usually ate supper and saved something for her.

Since she had seen her father stepping out, there had been a coolness in the household as if her parents were rooming at a boarding house. They rarely spent time together, and when they did, they suffered in silence.

Summer couldn't figure it out. *Was it the loss of his job? Was it the crush of bills? Did Mom already know? Should I say something? Would it send her over the edge?*

Summer's other issue was her boyfriend, Cyrus Tinkham. He pestered her to hang out. She had shut him down ever since she had stopped smoking weed.

I've got to keep a clear head. I don't need him. He's a waste.

They hadn't broken up, but he wasn't considered a priority. Summer knew Cyrus could always smoke with his younger brother, Marcus, and some buddies. She wondered if there wasn't a day of the week when Cyrus wasn't high. When Cyrus wasn't smoking weed, he was vaping.

Equipped with a license, Summer wanted to spend time with Gordon Beckwith, but geography was the problem. She had told him she'd be happy to drive to Tiot, but he said he'd think about it. Gordon had told her about his first girlfriend, Abbie Fortune, and Lizzie Soares, the intern from last summer.

On this Friday night, Summer pulled into her driveway by six o'clock. The traffic on the way home had been torturous. Her father's car and her mother's work van were gone. She stepped into the cool of the home and got changed. Mom was working in nearby Concord. Summer got changed and went into the kitchen.

She decided to whip something up for her and her mom.

Summer loved Italian food. She went with cacio pepe, an easy, delicious pasta dish. Summer got to work.

At seven o'clock, she heard her mother's van pull up. Melody strolled into the kitchen wearing paint-spattered jeans and a maroon-and-gold Boston College t-shirt.

She kissed her daughter on the cheek. "Smells nice. Where's Dad?"

"Don't know."

"His loss." Melody looked at the stove. "Do I have time to shower and get changed?"

"Sure."

Summer added a few final touches to the meal and checked on some buns in the oven. Melody reappeared with another Boston College t-shirt, a pair of white shorts, and sandals. Summer could almost pass as her mother's double except Mom's blond hair was straight, and she tanned easily.

"I'm starved."

"We're just about ready." Summer checked her pasta. The stove timer rang, and she pulled out the tray with the rolls.

"Any wine?" Mom asked.

"Saw some in the fridge."

Melody fetched a wine glass out of the cupboard and a bottle of white wine from the refrigerator.

"Would you like a glass, honey?"

"No thanks, Mom. Just water."

"I should, too, but a nice white wine with this meal would be perfect."

Summer dished out the food, put the buns on a small plate, poured herself some water, and sat down.

Her mother said, "Dear Lord, for what we are about to receive we thank you. Amen."

"Amen," replied Summer. Both made the sign of the cross. Summer hadn't gone to church in several years, much to her mother's chagrin.

They ate in quiet. After she finished, Melody said, "Thank you. That was yummy."

"It's easy to make."

Melody sipped her wine. "I have the feeling you want to tell me something."

"Do I?"

"I know you're not five years old anymore, but I can tell when you're about to make an announcement."

Summer cleared her throat. She said softly, "I saw Dad in Boston."

"Oh, nice."

"No, not nice. I saw him holding hands with another woman in the North End."

Melody sipped her wine. "It was his old boss, Kitty Kurver."

"Didn't she fire him?"

"Yes, Summer, but it wasn't her call."

Summer couldn't believe how calm her mother was.

"Aren't you pissed? Don't you want to smack him?"

Melody smiled. "This is nothing new with your father."

"My father's a cheater?"

"Yes."

Melody put out her right hand. "Hold on, dear. You can tarnish another halo."

"What do you mean?"

"I've cheated, too."

"Cut the shit! Both of you?"

"We've had an arrangement for years."

"Why didn't you get divorced? This is crazy!"

"We've stayed together because of you. We still love each other. Your dad will have his fun, but he always comes back to me."

"Wow. I never knew this."

"You've had a boyfriend for a few years, and you've been smoking dope. You've been oblivious. You had your own interests."

"I still can't believe this."

"Don't think anything less of us, Summer. We're still your parents; we still love you. We still want you to be happy."

Summer put up her hands. "My parents are swingers. Who would've believed it?"

"We're not swingers. We just have other interests."

Summer ate quietly. While she and her mother washed the dishes, Summer asked, "Are you keeping the Maine house?"

"Yup. I have a lot of jobs lined up. I might quit teaching and stick with this business. And I think Dad has a bite on a job. So, things may work out."

Summer still couldn't believe what she'd heard. The Maine house stays in the family while the two cheaters co-exist.

Thirty-two

Marty's Newest Addiction

Marty Beckwith had completed his diorama of the Battle of Saratoga in his man cave. Martin Keller, the owner of the local hobby shop, Game Time, called to ask if he could see his handiwork.

"Martin, how did you know of this?" asked Marty.

"Your son Gordon told me about your *Saratoga*. He told me how you and he toured the battlefield last fall and found the Benedict Arnold boot statue."

Marty smiled. *That was a good trip. Leave it to Gordon. I didn't know he visited Game Time.*

~ * ~

A day later, Martin sported a stringy beard, an old black Gollum t-shirt, a pair of stone cargo shorts, and tired brown sandals when he came over to the house. Marty brought him into his room.

"Man, this is fabulous!" he exclaimed. "Can I borrow it?"

"Come again?"

"Mr. Beckwith, I'd love to show this in my window display. I'll be very careful moving it."

"Ahh, I'm concerned it might get wrecked."

"Come down to the shop. I'll show you."

"I'd put up a sign announcing you as its creator. The detail is terrific. I love how you got Arnold on his horse ready to rally his troops."

"It's the decisive battle of the Revolution."

"Indeed."

The next day at noon, Marty drove over to Game Time. Martin showed him the store where he would display the diorama.

"Looks pretty safe, Martin." Marty walked around the store, checking out the games and models. He stopped at a model of the *U.S.S. Constitution.*

Martin leaned over to him. "Marty, have you done a ship model?" Marty shrugged.

"Tell you what. Loan me *Saratoga* for a month, and you can have a modeling kit of *Old Ironsides* for your next project."

"Deal. I just finished my son's book, *Six Frigates.*"

"Ian Toll, one of my favorite authors. Read his trilogy on the Navy in the Pacific in World War Two."

"I will. Thank you."

"No, thank you."

Gordon had gone out to a matinee movie with Moose Marini and, when he got home, he found his father busy with the shell of the *Constitution.*

"Now you're a ship builder, Dad."

"Thanks to you. I'm going to have to revisit *Old Ironsides.* I'm intrigued by this."

His father had laid out all the model's pieces on the table. "Maybe I can reconstruct one of the *Constitution*'s battles."

"The *HMS Guerriere?*"

"Of course, that's her most famous when it was declared that the *Constitution*'s sides were made of iron. I was thinking of her fighting against the *Cyane* and the *Levant* where she had to take on the two ships."

"That would be neat."

"Let me tackle the frigate first before the two smaller ships." His father picked up the directions. Then he sipped from his U-Maine mug, but the coffee had turned cold.

"How's Moose? I haven't seen him in a while."

"I swear he's getting bigger."

"Has he been lifting for football?"

"I think he's more successful lifting Twinkies."

Marty looked over the model's directions. "Moose still looking for a girlfriend?"

"Yeah, but no luck."

"Your love life has been quiet. No Abbie nor the lady from last summer. Well, you're a free man with no ties holding you down. I wish I had that in high school."

"You had a steady for most of high school?"

"Marilyn Kuberski, a lovely lady."

"What happened after high school graduation?"

"College." Gordon laughed. "I mean, we went to different schools. I headed out to Bangor; she went to Brown. We moved on."

"Did you keep in touch?"

"There was no social media, Gordo. I think I wrote one letter. Imagine someone nowadays sitting down to write a letter."

"Did she write you back?"

"A couple of times, but I got too much into hockey and partying."

"Did you regret losing the connection?"

"Not really. People grow up and move in different directions. Marilyn was a cheerleader, but she was a serious student, unlike me."

"Did you ever see her again?"

"At my twentieth high school reunion. She looked fabulous." Marty lifted his head and smiled. "But not as fabulous as your mother. She's a surgeon in Rhode Island."

"Wow."

"I was lucky to have her in my life and lucky to have known her."

"I don't think I'd have the time for a steady girlfriend, but I like the company. There is someone at work."

"You told me about her. She's a stoner."

"She's quit, but she lives far away."

"You'll have your license in the fall. That gal from last summer... she and you met a few times. If you really want to get together with this new girl, you'll be able to work it out."

"Maybe."

"Go ask your mother how long before supper."

"Sure, Dad."

Thirty-three

On His Case

Gordon's day didn't start off well.

First, when he woke up, he found his mother on the phone, and his father standing next to her.

Next, he heard his mother say, "Thank you, Doctor."

Gordon said, "What's up?"

"It's your grandmother," replied his dad.

"She took a fall and may have broken her hip," said his mother.

"Is she okay?" asked Gordon.

"I don't know, Gordon, but I'm leaving for Maine this morning to check on her. I may stay over if I have to."

"I'll go with you."

"No, go to work. I'll keep you and Dad updated."

Next, on the train into Boston, Gordon heard all about Abbie Fortune's new male interest, Victor Santos. She and Jack talked about Victor all the way into Boston. Gordon pretended to be reading, but between the news of his grandmother and Abbie's new guy he couldn't concentrate.

"He's a real good guy," Abbie said. "You two would like him. He's going to come out to Tiot next weekend."

Abbie and Jack continued until Jack and Gordon got off at Back Bay Station and switched to the Orange Line subway. They stood on the platform waiting for their train to North Station. Jack nudged Gordon.

"What's up with you, Gordon? Are you bummed by Abbie's new boyfriend?"

"No, my grandmother may have broken her hip. My mom is driving up to see her today."

"Sorry to hear that, man. Is she a nice lady?"

"I've just gotten to know her recently. I really like her."

The train pulled up and they stepped into the car. "Are you jealous about Abbie? C'mon, be honest."

"No. Well, maybe a little."

"It's your own fault. You didn't want to commit."

"Jack, we weren't going to get married. I've been busy."

"Really?" Jack smirked. "You two were inseparable freshman year."

"We've moved on."

"Have you?"

"Yes."

"What about Summer?"

"What about her?"

"She likes you. I don't know why she's not interested in me. I'm much better looking."

"C'mon, Jack. She lives too far away."

"She can drive now."

"I don't know."

As they stepped onto the North Washington Street Bridge, the boys looked to the right over to the Navy Yard.

When they got near the main entrance, Jack said, "Are you still on for lunch?"

"I think I'm just going to hang local."

Jack smiled. "You can tell Summer I'm available. Maybe she'll take a drive to see me. She'd have more fun with me."

Gordon waved Jack away.

Gordon and Summer both liked Emma as their immediate boss, but they had reservations about Benny Goodman. Emma was upbeat and positive. She was helpful and willing to answer questions. Benny barely acknowledged the two interns.

Gordon's bad mood continued when Benny asked to see him. No sooner had Gordon put down his backpack when Benny motioned for him to accompany him to his office.

"What were you doing with the chair of the trustees?"

Gordon was puzzled. "What?"

"What were you talking about with Clare Fairchild?"

"We were just talking. She asked me about my plans."

"She's the chairperson of the board of trustees for the museum."

"She told me."

"Why were you talking to her?"

"She almost fainted downstairs. I got her a water and took her outside to a bench. Is there a problem? I didn't know who she was."

"Did she mention me?"

"No. I didn't know who she was. She was very nice."

Benny grumbled to himself. Gordon couldn't catch what he said.

"Mr. Goodman, is there something wrong?"

Benny ruffled his beard and ran a hand over his head.

"I think they're trying to get rid of me. That's all. My job is on the line. If you want to keep your job, you better watch your step."

Gordon was confused. He had only been trying to help someone who almost fainted.

Why is Benny Goodman on my case? He barely acknowledges me.

"Okay, get the hell out of my office." Gordon stood up. "Wait. Mitch said you had been on the *Cassin Young* recently, and he couldn't find you."

"I was on my lunch break. I was just on the main deck."

Benny pointed at him. "There's something different about you, Gordon Beckwith. I don't know what is, but I will find out. Dismissed."

Gordon slowly departed. For the rest of the day, he delivered supplies to the store, swept floors, and removed trash.

He started to leave for the day when Summer grabbed him.

"Gordon, wait up."

"What's going on?"

"What do you mean?"

"I didn't see your usual smiling self this afternoon. Something wrong?"

"My grandmother broke her hip, and Benny Goodman gave me a hard time for helping a lady I thought was going to faint."

"You were being helpful."

"How was I to know she's the head honcho of the museum, and the chair of the board of the trustees. He was acting real paranoid. He told me to stay away from her."

"That sucks. I'm really sorry about your grandmother."

"Thanks."

They stopped at Summer's Jeep. "Gordon, could we hang out sometime outside of work?"

"I don't have a license."

She waved her car key at him. "I do."

"You want to drive to scenic Tiot?"

"My parents were going to sell the Wells place in the fall. Now, they're not. They rented it out. But I haven't gone to Maine all summer."

She unlocked her vehicle. "Hey, I've got an idea. Why don't we take a ride to Ogunquit? You've been there?"

"Nope. What's up with Ogunquit?"

"Maybe the most beautiful beach in New England."

"I'm not much of a beach person."

"Trust me. There's the Marginal Way, a great walk along the water. I'll pick you up at home, and we'll head up early on a Saturday."

Gordon thought about it. *A beautiful girl offers to take me for a ride.*

"Tell you what. Let me check with my dad. I don't think he needs me Saturday. You can meet me at a commuter rail station north of Boston, so you don't do a lot of driving."

"I can do that. We'll talk some more tomorrow."

Summer jumped in and started the car. Jack Quincy ambled down the street to meet Gordon. Summer pulled away and waved at the two boys.

Jack said, "Gordon, you have a funny look on your face."

"Jack, I was having a crappy day, but now a pretty girl wants to drive me to some beach in Maine."

"Cut the crap, Gordon. I wish I was you." Jack punched him on the shoulder "I'm still better looking than you."

Thirty-four

Beach Bound

"You're lucky, I didn't need you this weekend, Gordon," said his father on their ride to Boston's North Station. From there, Gordon would take the commuter train to Newburyport, close to the New Hampshire line.

Marty had decided Gordon's original attempt to connect with Summer Atkins was too complicated. Gordon would have had to ride two different commuter trains. Dropping Gordon at North Station would eliminate one rail trip. North Station and South Station are situated about a mile apart with no rail link.

"I appreciate the ride, Dad."

"You couldn't go out with a local girl like Abbie. You had the gal from last summer who lived in Plymouth. Now, you have another who lives in the other direction."

"I can't wait to get my license."

"It can't come soon enough." Marty chuckled.

Saturday morning, Marty's blue Ford truck pulled up in front of North Station. Gordon grabbed his gear. He stepped out.

Marty rolled down his window. "I hope this lady is a safe driver, and she's not smoking weed."

"Dad, I wouldn't get into a car with anyone like that."

"Okay, what am I going to say to you?"

"Be a gentleman. Always treat women with respect."

Marty laughed. "Good. You listened."

Marty gave Gordon fifty bucks. "Thanks, Dad. You didn't have to. I am working."

He hugged his son. "Have a great time. Don't get sunburned. Your mother will be mad."

Gordon waved and headed into the station.

Waiting for the train, Gordon stepped into the Boston Bruins gift shop. He studied the jerseys of the former Boston greats: Bobby Orr, Johnny Bucyk, Ray Bourque, and Cam Neely.

He bought an Orr t-shirt and stashed it in his Bruins backpack.

I would love to play pro hockey here. It would be even greater to play for the Bruins.

He laughed. *First, I better worry about playing for the University of Maine Black Bears.*

On the train platform, he waited for five minutes before the train shuffled to a stop. Since he lived west of Boston, Gordon enjoyed seeing new sights on the way north to Newburyport.

When he stepped off the train, he saw a pretty girl with blonde curls sitting on the hood of a yellow Jeep.

Summer asked, "Were you worried I wouldn't be here?"

"No, I wasn't."

"Hop in."

Summer steered them to Route 95 toward New Hampshire and Maine.

"I know this part of the road."

"I've known it since I was a kid. I love Maine. Maybe, I'll move here when I get older."

"From what I've seen, I like it."

"But you haven't been to Ogunquit."

"No, I've gone to Orono and to Bath."

"U-Maine in Orono. What's in Bath?"

"My mother grew up there. My grandmother still lives there."

Summer drove the speed limit and stayed in the right lane. She wore sunglasses and a pair of denim shorts. Gordon tried not to stare at her legs.

They crossed the bridge over the Piscatagua River from Portsmouth, New Hampshire into Kittery, Maine. Summer pulled over to the rest stop in Kittery. They got out to the use the bathrooms, got back into the vehicle, and exited out the back onto Route 1.

Summer said, "Let's cut the AC and roll down the windows."

"Sure."

The teens breezed north through Kittery, York, and into Ogunquit. Gordon noticed the increased traffic on Route 1 heading into Ogunquit.

"A popular place," said Gordon.

"Exactly."

They made it into the center and headed down to the beach.

"Forty bucks to park?" asked Gordon.

"Yup. Look at the lot. It's how the town makes its money."

Gordon saw it was almost filled up with vehicles. He grabbed his wallet and produced the money.

"I've got this," said Summer. "My treat."

"You're driving. You paid for your gas."

Summer smiled. "You can buy me an ice cream later."

"Sure."

She handed her money to the attendant and parked the car. Summer opened the back and pointed to two beach chairs. She strapped one on her back. Gordon followed suit and carried his backpack in his arms. The tide was out, so there was plenty of room to put down roots.

After they opened the chairs, she shunned her t-shirt and shorts, leaving her with a pink bikini.

"Want to go in first?" asked Summer. They walked down to the shore, and she ran in and dove into a wave.

Gordon dipped his foot into the clear water. "It's cold."

Summer surfaced. "You get used to it."

She walked toward him, grabbed his hand, and they raced into the water. When they reached thigh-height, Summer dove into another incoming wave. Gordon marveled at the frothiness as the waves crashed.

"C'mon," she waved. "It gets better."

"It's freezing."

"Don't be a baby. You play hockey. Cold shouldn't be a problem."

Summer splashed Gordon with both hands.

"Okay, okay."

He jumped in. "I'm still cold."

"You'll get used to it."

While Gordon was swimming, several motorboats cruised by, but he felt no desire to set foot on a boat.

Summer and Gordon rode the waves. Gordon couldn't believe how strong the current was and how clean the water was. Several of the waves carried him into shallow water and soon he forgot the cold.

After an hour in the water, they walked back to the chairs. Summer took out a blanket and stretched out.

"I'm gonna chill. You can join me."

Gordon wasn't comfortable with her offer. "I brought a book."

"I'm not surprised."

Summer conked out. Gordon slathered sunscreen over himself and put his t-shirt back on. He put on his sunglasses and sat down to inspect Ogunquit Beach. Hundreds of kids, parents, and lovers frolicked in the surf while others snoozed or kept to their reading. He noticed the Ogunquit River flowed into the corner of the beach. Bathers and paddle boarders floated on the river current.

Summer awoke later and produced peanut butter and jelly sandwiches and two water bottles.

"What do you think?" she asked with a smear of jelly at the corner of her mouth. Gordon leaned over and wiped it away with a finger.

"Fantastic beach. This is the best sandwich ever." Summer shook her head in disbelief.

"You ain't seen nothing yet, Gordon. Look to your right in front of the motels. See those people walking up above? That's the Marginal Way. We'll walk that to Perkins Cove. It's my favorite place to walk."

After lunch, Summer returned to the blanket, Gordon to his book. He reapplied more sunscreen and put on a blue Red Sox cap.

They jumped back into the water for a few minutes, returned to their spot, and folded up camp as the tide marched to shore. After putting the beach supplies into the Jeep, they washed off the sand at the showers outside of the restrooms.

Summer's hair seemed even curlier. "Now, we walk."

They took a shortcut to the Shore Road and headed for the start of the Marginal Way a few blocks away. The sidewalks groaned with the weight of tourists. Cars filled up Shore Road. Shoppers ducked in and out of stores. Motels abounded. They reached a motel called the Sparhawk and found the start of the path. As they started, Summer pointed to the explosion of flowers adorning the right side of the walk. Gordon also saw the beach in the distance.

"This is one of my favorite views. The Sparhawk Motel's flowers are amazing."

Summer shot several pictures with her phone. Gordon did, too.

They rounded the bend past several other motels where guests sat in Adirondack chairs overlooking the splendor. The pedestrian traffic, at times, only allowed single-file movement. Gordon followed Summer. As they progressed along the trail, the ocean in its beauty hugged them on the left side. Jetties had been formed with narrow beaches hidden between the rocks.

The Marginal Way was thronged with folks, but they didn't mind. Some of the homes had been part of the scenery for years.

One residence looked newer, like it wasn't an original structure. It featured gray stone with two dormers.

"Look at this place," said Gordon as he pointed to his right. They stopped at its black wrought-iron gate. Bushes ringed the back border of the property. A large bird feeder capped by copper invited flying guests.

"I love that place," replied Summer. "I'd love to explore it. I wonder if the owners just use it in the good weather."

"All these homes face the ocean."

"Gordon, you could eat breakfast and enjoy the waves."

At that, a blonde woman walked out of the gray house. She held a coffee mug in her hand and headed for a beach chair in the back yard. Gordon and Summer stood just outside of her hedges.

She shouted, "Gordon?"

"Mrs. Fairchild?" he yelled back.

She wore white shorts, a pink jersey with pearls, and a white visor.

"You two please come over into the yard."

They entered through the gate. The three of them sat underneath a pink beach umbrella.

Mrs. Fairchild said, "Would you like something to drink? Soda? Water? Coffee? Tea?" She lifted her mug. "I know it's warm out, but I enjoy a hot coffee."

"If you have water, Mrs. Fairchild."

"Sure, Gordon. Summer?"

"Water's good, too. Thank you."

Their hostess slipped away.

Summer punched Gordon on the arm. "You've never been to Ogunquit, and you know somebody. I've come here for years and never met anyone." She laughed. "I saw you checking out her legs."

Gordon blushed.

Mrs. Fairchild returned with two bottles of Poland Springs. "Here we are. Water from the good state of Maine."

The kids opened their bottles and sipped.

Mrs. Fairchild chuckled. "I'm cynical about the spring water."

"Why's that?" asked Gordon.

"I think all these outfits that tout authentic spring water use the same tap as the others." She smiled.

She cupped her mug with her hands. "I told Gordon I had a place in Ogunquit. What do you think of my humble summer home?"

Summer said, "Breathtaking. We have a place in Wells, but I'd take this as my permanent home."

"Unbelievable," Gordon said.

She waved them inside for a quick tour. First, she showed them the second floor. Her bedroom and one guest bedroom overlooked the water. The other two bedrooms were decked out in nautical themes. On the main floor there was a large dining room, a white kitchen, a black Steinway piano, and the living room facing the Atlantic.

Summer walked into a guest room that faced the water. There was a painting, a portrait of a young man. She looked at it quickly.

She muttered, "Holy shit!"

Gordon saw Summer put her hands to her mouth.

"What's the matter?"

"Look at this painting."

Gordon looked. "What, Summer?"

"Gordon, he looks like you except his hair is a little darker. It must be her son."

Mrs. Fairchild had caught up with them. "Ah, you found my favorite painting. My son Jeremy was killed years ago. Like you, Gordon, he was a hockey player, a damn good one. They had won a big game. He got into a car with an older player who drove recklessly. The driver survived; Jeremy did not. He was sixteen, my only child with Mr. Fairchild. So, Summer, he does look a lot like Gordon."

She straightened the picture frame. "I'll meet you outside."

They sat in lawn chairs and Mrs. Fairchild said, "Thank you for visiting me. If you're around for supper, you can join me. My personal chef can whip up anything."

"Thank you, Mrs. Fairchild, but we'll probably be heading back home," said Summer.

The teens returned to the Marginal Way, even more crowded than earlier.

Gordon said, "You didn't want stay for supper? She seems lonely."

"I agree, but that painting really spooked me. Besides, Mr. Beckwith, we haven't gone for the best ice cream in Maine."

"Where's that?'

"Big Daddy's in Wells, just up the road."

Gordon shot a lot of pictures as they headed into Perkins Cove, flocked with sail and fishing boats. A white pedestrian bridge loomed over the cove. When they reached it, they stopped at a store to buy two waters, sat on a bench overlooking the boats, walked on the bridge, and headed back on the Marginal Way enroute to the beach. When they got back to the parking lot, most of the shore was close to being submerged by the incoming tide. They jumped into Summer's vehicle.

She asked, "What did you think, Gordon?"

Gordon surveyed the waves and all the bathers. "Fantastic. I've never been to a beach like this. I had gone to Nantasket a few times with my mother, but this is great. I'll have to come back."

Fifteen minutes later, they sat at a picnic table working on individual hot fudge sundaes. Gordon wiped whipped cream off Summer's cheek and chuckled. "This is a good substitute for supper."

"Our place in Wells is nearby, but we should head for home. It's a long ride."

As they progressed from Maine to New Hampshire to Massachusetts, Gordon and Summer said little and listened to music. When she passed the Newburyport exit, Gordon said, "I thought you were going to drop me back there."

"I'll drive you to South Station. That way it's only one train ride home."

Finally, they arrived at the station. She leaned over and kissed him.

"Thanks for coming," she said. "I had a great time."

"Thanks for inviting me," he answered.

"We'll have to do this again sometime. You're good company."

"You, too, Summer."

On the train ride home, Gordon left his book in his backpack and recalled the day's events. He felt sorry for Mrs. Fairchild losing her only child and he wished Summer lived closer.

Why do I like girls who live far away?

Thirty-five

Benny on the Hunt

Benny Goodman had a lousy weekend, but at least he wasn't hungover. He had imposed upon himself a ban on all liquor. He was devoted to his mission to get into shape.

His ex-wife, Tovah, called him on Saturday morning to tell him she was marrying Patty O'Connell, his old girlfriend. That hurt.

Then he tried to play tennis with a neighbor and hurt his back. By Sunday, he was almost able to stand up straight and contemplated seeing a chiropractor.

Sunday night, he trolled a few dating apps, but those websites depressed him even more. He hadn't had a date in years.

He woke up Monday morning still with a stiff lower back and a headache. Benny couldn't believe how crappy he felt. Maybe physical therapy might work out better, he thought.

When he arrived at work at the *Constitution* Museum, Mrs. Clare Fairchild sat in his battered chair.

"Good morning, Benjamin," she said.

Her greeting jolted him from any drowsiness.

What is she doing here? A trustee shouldn't be sitting in my chair.

"Have you had breakfast?" she asked.

"Just some orange juice."

"Are you okay?"

Benny put his work bag on the desk. "My ex is getting married, and I threw out my back trying to play tennis. It's not a hangover."

"I'm sorry to hear that. How about I take you out for breakfast?"

"I had some reports to go over this morning."

"C'mon, I know a nice place in Somerville."

The chairwoman's Mercedes silver SUV was parked outside the door. She drove. Benny's headache had just started to subside.

I can't believe this. Why is she here? Is she going to threaten me? Is she trying to fire me?

The ride to the restaurant took twenty minutes. To Benny, it looked like a townie hangout, nothing special.

She ordered an omelet. He went with scrambled eggs, sausage, and home fries. Each drank coffee.

Clare said, "I had the unexpected pleasure of seeing your two interns on Saturday at my place in Ogunquit."

Benny was really confused. *Huh? What is she talking about?*

"I'm sorry. You saw the two kids, our interns? Were they invited?"

"Oh, no, they happened to be in Ogunquit and went for a walk on the Marginal Way. I was sitting in the back yard of my summer home when they walked by. It was nice of them to spend some time with an old lady."

Benny thought: *Mrs. Fairchild doesn't look that old. She may have had surgery and taken botox.* He found her very attractive for her age.

"I hope they're doing a good job."

"Oh, sure. I delegated most of their supervision to Emma Wollensky."

"There's something special about that Gordon."

What is it about that kid? He's a pain in the ass.

They ate their meals in silence. She said, "I liked your idea of a campaign about the ghosts at the Navy Yard. We could top it off with a special event near Halloween. Invite children to dress in costume and visit both ships. I appreciate your creativity. You may know some ghost stories from your research about the yard."

"There are a few."

"You can work them into the website and into any promotional literature, or it might be something Emma could do with your input."

Benny sipped his coffee and nodded.

"Any progress on your book about the Navy Yard?" Benny almost choked on a piece of sausage. For the past two years, he had ignored the book.

"It's getting there."

"It would give the museum some cachet if our Harvard grad director wrote a book about our national park. Maybe you need to take a leave of absence to really tackle the project."

"Oh, I can handle the job and the book."

Benny whipped out his debit card, but Mrs. Fairchild's right hand patted his hand.

"It's on me, Benny. I dragged you away."

The chair of the trustees said, "I'm glad we've had some time together. Stay well and keep up the good work."

Benny thanked her for the breakfast. When she dropped him off, he felt better than he had over the weekend. He was still concerned about Gordon Beckwith. He knew he couldn't fire him for any good reason. Emma liked him as well, but there was something about him. *What really had happened when Gordon visited the* Cassin *Young?*

Thirty-six

DD 793

Gordon wasn't used to moodiness. It didn't sit well with him. Calamities washed over him, but he was worried about this grandmother who wasn't well, and his mother who was trying to cope with the possible loss of her mother.

He also was saddened by the fact that Abbie Fortune was going out with another guy, but he was happy she was happy. Their train rides with Jack Quincy showed the glow in her blue eyes when she talked about working in Boston and spending time with Victor Santos.

Gordon liked Summer Atkins, but the physical distance between their homes served as a barrier. Their day in Maine had been an unexpected pleasure. Other than seeing Summer at work, getting together would require more creative thinking. Maybe when he got his license, Gordon could see her in Acton. But it wasn't like he could just drop in and hang out with her like he could with Abbie.

Gordon was worried about his mother. Martha wasn't herself. Worry and exhaustion had plagued her since her mother took ill. Gray circles resided below her eyes. Gordon noticed crow's feet carved into the corner of her eyes. Her husband tried to keep up his wife's spirits.

Summer detected Gordon wasn't himself this Monday morning. They sat on a bench outside the museum overlooking the dry dock and the *U.S.S. Cassin Young*. To their right, tourists queued up in line to step onto *Old Ironsides*. The mid-morning broke out shafts of sunlight.

"How was your weekend, Gordon?" she asked.

"Quiet. I worked at my father's liquor store."

"You've been very quiet this morning."

"My grandmother is dying."

She touched his shoulder. "I'm so sorry."

"Thanks. I feel bad for my mother. She was the baby of the family, and she doesn't see her siblings. Her father has been gone for a while."

"Where is she, your grandmother?'

"I've told you she lives in Bath, Maine where my mom grew up."

"I've never been there."

"It's a pretty cool place, famous for ship building. I've gone up a couple of times this year and spent time with my grandmother."

"Do you like her?'

"I do. The funny thing is that she and my dad haven't gotten along."

"Why's that?"

"My grandmother envisioned my mother ending up with her high school boyfriend. He was the valedictorian; Mom was the salutatorian."

"What happened?"

"They went to different colleges, and that was that."

"The guy's probably married with kids."

Gordon chuckled. "Ironically, he made a lot of money, returned home, and is now the mayor. My grandmother worked for his campaign. I've met him. He's still a bachelor."

"Nice guy?"

"Seems to be. He is a politician. I think he still likes my mother."

"That must've been awkward."

"It was. I feel bad about my father. He didn't fit my grandmother's dream for her daughter."

Gordon checked his watch. "We should be getting back."

"Hey, Gordon, what's up with Benny Goodman?"

Gordon sipped some Gatorade. "What do you mean?"

"He's different. He's cleaned up his act. He talks to us."

"It is weird."

"Any idea about the change?"

"Haven't a clue."

"I don't buy it. He usually treated us like he got something bad stuck on his shoe, and now he's Mr. Sunshine. I still don't trust him."

Thirty-seven

The Big Decision

Mark Preston was crazy about Claudia Gomes, the state library director. This woman was beautiful and brilliant. He admitted to himself that Claudia was much smarter than he. They had been seeing each other for a year. When they met, Claudia was emerging from a divorce. The first few months of their relationship saw weekly dates. His availability was limited due to his schedule. He spent a lot of his time after work time giving speeches throughout the state. His public service TV ads about voter registration and the other responsibilities of the secretary of state were aired constantly on the local TV stations. This was his life.

He had just hit fifty, yet his hair remained untainted by gray or thinning. Daily gym workouts and golf kept his waistline trim. They were necessary to counter his addiction to chocolate.

For most of his life, he had never thought seriously about marriage. Mark Preston wasn't sure if he was in love with this woman. If he ran for governor, should there be a beautiful woman by his side? Would Claudia want to be remarried? Would she want to be pestered by the press? What if she turned him down?

She was a private person and turned down numerous offers to accompany him on various appearances. The subject of marriage or living together had never been brought up.

"That's not me," she told him several times. "Working as the head of the state library is about as public as I want to be. You've done well as a solo for years. You don't need me."

At first, Mark was disappointed, but he respected her wishes. He would be out pressing the flesh with voters while she sat in the background. The governor's office remained his goal.

As a boy, young Mark dedicated his energies to sports. As a young man, he had served his country in the Marines. Returning home, he knew his path to a political career required an education, so he commuted to the University of Massachusetts in Boston. After graduation, he studied law at Suffolk University. He worked several jobs to support himself. He briefly prosecuted criminal cases as an assistant district attorney, but the law didn't hold the allure of political office. Then in his thirties, Mark ran for state representative and won. He possessed the natural gifts of a politician. He remembered people's names, he looked them in the eye, gave a firm handshake, and offered a toothpaste smile. The spotlight welcomed him.

Once in office, his mission was to become governor of the Commonwealth of Massachusetts. As a state rep, he sat on several committees. He was considered a moderate who got along with his fellow Democrats and the Republicans.

At thirty-eight years of age, an opportunity had opened up. The incumbent secretary of state retired, and Mark decided to run for state office. Get his name known out of metropolitan Boston. Winning might be the springboard to the big office. He ran unopposed as a Democrat and easily defeated the Republican candidate in the final election. Since then, he had faced only token opposition for reelection.

Should he get married prior to his gubernatorial run? How would the media treat it? Unlike some politicians, Mark found the press useful. He tried to be upfront and truthful.

He decided to bring the marriage debate up with his deputy, Doc Ott. Mark asked Ott to step into his office this morning.

"Doc, close the door."

Ott wondered what was up. His boss rarely closed the door with him.

"Doc, I'm looking for guidance."

Ott couldn't imagine why he wanted help. Mark pretty much delegated most of the office's daily functions to Ott.

"I was thinking about asking Claudia Gomes to be my wife. Do you think this is a good move?"

Ott smiled. "Are you doing this to enhance your candidacy, or because you really want this lady in your life?"

Mark grinned. "Maybe both."

"I would lean on your heart. Is she more important to you than being governor?"

"That's a toss-up."

"It shouldn't be."

"Doc, if you couldn't have both, could you pick one over the other?" asked his boss.

"At this point in my life, Mark, I would pick which one would make me happier. I never wanted to be governor."

Preston knew his deputy had been going out with a woman, a librarian who worked for Claudia.

Preston picked up a David Ortiz-autographed baseball from his desk and tossed it in the air. "You've been seeing that librarian, Esther Kanon."

"Yes."

"Is marriage in the cards?"

"She's divorced; I've been a bachelor my whole life. I think we like the current arrangement."

"But you were engaged once?"

Ott couldn't remember if he had ever told Mark Preston that story, or if he had learned about it from another source.

"Yes, Mark," he said slowly. Emotions he kept inside for years started to bubble over. "And I killed her while driving drunk. I've lived with that every day. She was my true love."

Tears dribbled down his cheeks. Ott removed his rimless glasses and wiped his face. "I'm sorry."

"Don't be, Doc."

They sat without words for a minute. After wiping his eyes, Doc returned to his role as the guidance counselor. "Time for real politics. If you decide to pop the question and run for governor, Mark, is there anything from your past that might come back to bite you in the ass?"

Now it was Mark's turn to dredge up the past. "When I got of the service and went to U-Mass Boston and then Suffolk Law School, I dated a girl. She was lovely, a nursing student. And—"

"And what?" Doc expected bad news.

"She told me she was pregnant."

Ott sat on the edge of his chair. "What happened?"

"I told her to get an abortion. I was so consumed with my career; my folks had just died. I couldn't handle it. Was it really my child? What if she secretly had been seeing other guys on the side when she went out with me? She was very Catholic. She looked at me with such hate and scooted away. I never saw her again."

"Do you know where she is now?"

"I don't. I haven't thought about her till recently."

"For God's sakes, Mark, with your job, you have all kinds of information at your disposal to find her. If you ran for governor, you've never thought to track her down? What if she had the child? Wouldn't you want to know?"

"Doc, I was very selfish and moved on. It wasn't my finest hour."

"Jesus, Mark, you are a cold-hearted son of a bitch."

"I'm not proud of myself. I like to consider myself a good person. It's what my dad would've wanted. Back then, I was going to classes, bartending, and just wanted to have some fun."

Doc Ott ran a hand over his white curls. "Have you told Claudia about this?"

"No, I've been too embarrassed."

"You may be ambushed if this got out to the press. She may not want to marry you if you weren't truthful. She may consider you untrustworthy."

"She may."

"What're going to do, boss?"

Mark stood and started to pace. "I guess I'll have to tell her about it and see what she says."

"Also, you should try to track down this lady from your past who may be the mother of your child. Wouldn't you want to know if you had a son or a daughter?"

"Doc, I probably would. All these years all I've only thought about was me."

"All I can say, Mark, is you better think about Claudia, and whether or not you should run for governor. What do you want the most?"

Mark scratched his head and exhaled. "I don't know. I've worked all these years toward that one goal. I've always depended on myself. I'm an only child; my parents have been gone for years. If I don't get married, will I miss what I've never had?"

Doc got up slowly. "Do you want power, or do you want love? I don't know if you can possess both."

"Thanks, Doc, for listening. I hope you don't think less of me."

"I don't. None of us is perfect."

Mark walked over to his deputy and shook his hand. "I'm glad you have someone in your life."

Doc Ott put a hand on his boss's shoulder. "I hope you can keep one in yours."

Thirty-eight

Father Issues

Abbie Fortune had a father issue; Victor Santos did, too. Abbie knew her dad; Victor had never known his father's identity. Sometimes Victor wondered if he had been the product of a random donor. That would be weird. He didn't think so.

They saw each other every day at work, but the two hadn't reconnected for a second outing.

While waiting for her mother in the state library, Abbie said to Victor before he left for day, "Why don't we meet here in town instead of you going to Tiot?"

Victor brightened. "Sure. Where?"

"The swan boats."

"What? Those goofy boats with the wooden swans the tourists all ride? Toss breadcrumbs to the ducks and pigeons?"

"Yes, those goofy things."

If Victor wanted to see Abbie again away from work, he'd suffer the embarrassment of the swan boats. Skinny probably would laugh at him. Plus, he'd had never been to Tiot.

"Victor, have you ever gone on one of them?"

"No."

"C'mon. We can walk around the Public Garden. It's a beautiful spot. You like to draw."

He was puzzled. This idea didn't seem like a lot of fun, but he wanted to spend more time with this girl.

"Okay. When and where?"

"How about this Saturday? We can meet by the George Washington statue."

"Where's that?"

She giggled "Victor, Washington sits on his charger by the Arlington Street entrance of the Public Garden. You can't miss him high atop the base of the statue."

"Okay, I can do that. What will we do after that?"

"Maybe the swan boats. Maybe not. We'll go wherever the wind blows."

Victor told Gus Saunders about this plan on the way home.

"Victor, what's the problem?" asked Gus.

"The swan boats?"

Gus shook his head. "Go with it. You want to spend time with this lady. Go along to get along."

"She's a straight girl. Some of the girls from school like to smoke weed, drink, and party."

"Maybe that doesn't float her boat. You had a good time with her the first time. Right?" Victor nodded. "Enjoy your time with her. Who cares what you do! She likes being with you. You don't have to get high to have a good time. I learned that a long time ago."

"I guess you're right."

"I know I'm right. Be open to new things. Some experiences may surprise you."

Gus's car pulled up in his driveway. Victor slouched out of the passenger seat.

Gus stepped out and leaned on the hood. "Something else bothering you?"

"Gus, did you know your father?"

"Yes, I did."

"Was he a good father?"

Gus straightened up and walked next to Victor. "He put food in my belly and put a roof over my head. For that, I'm appreciative."

"Was he good to you?"

"I learned a lot of lessons about life from him."

"So, he was a wise man?"

"No, he was a son-of-a-bitch drunk who beat my mother." Old feelings started to rumble. "When, I got older, I stopped his anger. I told him never to lay his hands on her. And he stopped. The old man finally quit the booze and found God. He wasn't a bad guy after that. Let me tell you, for years our home was a battlefield.

"I know it's different with no dad around for you, but your mom is doing her best for you. Nobody in the world loves you more than your mother. You may think she's tough. She has to be to get by in this crazy world." Gus pointed at Victor. "Do not take her for granted."

Victor nodded and headed inside.

~ * ~

The next morning Abbie ate breakfast with her mother. "What's up with Dad? I haven't seen or heard from him in a long time."

"New baby, new wife. That takes up a lot of time and energy."

"You're defending your ex-husband, the man who deserted you for five years?" Abbie's face started to redden.

Claudia had been quietly eating grapefruit and sipping tea before Abbie's outburst.

"Abbie, I'm not defending him. I'm speculating."

"I thought he was going to teach me how to drive."

"He told me he plans to. I think I'd be too nervous teaching you to drive. You can go visit him, Theresa, and the baby."

"I don't have a license."

"I can drop you off, and Dad drive you home."

Abbie rubbed her chin. "Maybe. I'll think about it."

Next morning, Claudia dropped Abbie off at the train station. Abbie kept thinking about Jack Fortune on the way into Boston and when she stepped off the train.

How could he have left us back then? I know he had a serious gambling addiction, but not to know if he was even alive wasn't fair to us.

Those thoughts pervaded her mind on the walk from Back Bay Station to the Public Garden. Abbie stopped at the back of the Washington statue and surveyed her surroundings. A lady in a violet dress played violin to her left with her instrument case open on the ground. On her right, Abbie saw a swan boat peddled by a wedding party posing for pictures near the edge of the lagoon. She turned to admire the flowers and plants encircling the Founding Father. She looked up to see to Victor Santos walking across the tiny suspension bridge.

"Hey," he said. "There's a long line for the swan boats."

"You know what? I don't feel like waiting. Do you want to walk to the Gardner Museum?"

"Where's that?"

"In the Fenway. It's an art museum."

"Sure." Victor almost exhaled with relief from not having to go on the swan boats.

The teens exited the Public Garden, crossed Arlington Street, and slowly strolled along the Commonwealth Avenue Mall, the pedestrian walkway that coursed down the middle of the street. The old tall trees afforded plenty of shade.

Holding hands, they walked slowly, stopped at various sculptures, and gawked at the different buildings along the way. Some of them were residences; some were business offices.

"Man, I've never been over here," he said, scanning the structures, mostly constructed in the late 1800s. "These dudes must have a lot of money."

"I think so. They probably had butlers, cooks, and nannies."

The streets intersecting Commonwealth Avenue ran in alphabetical order: Arlington, Berkeley, Clarendon, Dartmouth, Exeter, Fairfield. Gloucester, and Hereford.

Abbie identified most of the people who were commemorated in stone: John Glover, Revolutionary War fighter from Marblehead, Alexander Hamilton (before he became a musical), and Patrick Collins, an Irish-American Boston mayor.

"How do you know all this?' asked Victor.

"I read the inscriptions on the monuments and looked them up on the internet. I'm a library geek, Victor."

They reached a dark and shiny memorial for firefighters lost in a horrible fire at the nearby Hotel Vendome. A single fireman's helmet rested atop his coat. In 1972, a total of nine Boston firemen had lost their lives in that blaze.

As they progressed along the Commonwealth Mall, they passed woman suffragist Lucy Stone, former First Lady Abigail Adams, and former slave and poet, Phyllis Wheatley. They stopped to gaze at William Lloyd Garrison, abolitionist editor of the *Liberator*, Boston naval historian Samuel E. Morison, and explorer Leif Eriksson.

Victor laughed. "I feel like I'm in history class, Abbie, but it's more fun with you."

Abbie guided them toward Hereford Street. From there, they turned left onto Hereford, walked two blocks, and turned right onto Boylston Street.

Victor kept his head on a swivel. "How do you know where you're going?"

"Remember, my mother's a librarian, and we love museums. C'mon."

She took Victor's hand and pointed out the Berklee School of Music, the Massachusetts Historical Society, the Massachusetts Turnpike, and other landmarks. The teens made it to Park Drive, passed the Museum of Fine Arts on their left, and around the bend finally to the Gardner. Abbie used passes from the Tiot Library to reduce their prices of admission.

"What is this place?" he asked.

She replied, "It's a place of enchantment. One person put this together: she bought the land, oversaw its construction, acquired the art, and placed it where she wanted it."

"Who?"

"Isabella Stewart Gardner."

"She must have been crazy rich."

Abbie laughed. "Yes, she had to be. She took a trip to Italy when she was a teenager and told a friend she wanted to build a palazzo crammed with art."

"She must've had crazy money."

"Mrs. Gardner was never poor. She married money, and she came from money."

They entered the Gardner through the modern entrance and shuffled to its courtyard decked out with flowers and vines. Victor scanned the courtyard and looked up at the other three floors.

"One rich lady lived in this place?" he asked.

"For the most part, by herself, a widow. Her husband and young son had already died."

"Abbie, this place is like hundred times larger than my house in Mattapan."

"Same here." She dragged Victor over to her favorite painting by John Singer Sargent, "El Jaleo," a painting of a lady dancing the flamenco in front of musicians that spread out along the wall. The painting measured about seven and half feet by eleven feet.

"What does 'El Jaleo' mean? My Spanish isn't that great. My mom is fluent, but she always preached speaking English."

"I think it means 'the ruckus.'"

"Sure looks like it. This painting is crazy. This lady is hypnotic. I wish I could paint something like this."

"Maybe you will someday."

"Not that size," he replied with a smile. "I'll stick with my sketching."

Abbie and Victor made their way and slowly climbed the stairs.

Victor said, "I wish we could take pictures. Some of this stuff is fantastic. I just draw. These are phenomenal paintings."

"There are several nice pictorial books on the Gardner."

When they got to the Dutch Room on the second floor, two empty frames hung from the wall.

"What's up with these?" he queried. "How come there are no paintings hung there?"

Abbie responded. "March 18, 1990. The greatest unsolved art museum robbery."

"Unsolved?"

"Couple of guys dressed as cops slipped in after hours and made off with several valuable pieces of art. The crooks are still out there. Maybe worth a hundred million. There's a documentary on Netflix."

"I'll definitely check it out."

After two hours of inspection, Victor asked for a break for a drink. They headed to the cafeteria. Abbie drank tea and Victor a Coke.

Victor was so immersed in the visit he almost forgot he was touring with another person. Each teen devoured a bag of potato chips.

"Abbie, this is a wild place. You've got plants and flowers on the first floor, statues everywhere, and paintings galore. And she lived in this place?"

"Yes. Mrs. Gardner. She staged concerts, boxing matches, and she was a big Red Sox fan. If your name is Isabella, you got in for free."

Victor sipped his Coke. "As much as I like the place, I'm not changing my name to Isabella."

She chuckled. "Had enough?"

"I think so, but I'd come back."

"Next time we can visit the MFA, which dwarfs the Gardner."

"I'd like that. This place is cool. Thanks for taking me."

"No problem. It was my pleasure.

Along Huntington Avenue, they walked slowly hand in hand to Ruggles Station next to Northeastern University. When they got there, Abbie and Victor were pooped. Victor bought two waters while they waited for their respective trains.

"Victor, thanks for a great time."

"Well, thanks for taking me to the Gardner. It was sick."

Abbie checked the large digital marquee for her train's arrival. "My train's here."

Victor walked her to the platform. She kissed him quickly, waved, and scurried away.

Victor watched her slide into a car. *Who cares if Abbie's not a party girl? She's very cool and pretty.*

Thirty-nine

Benny's Paranoia

Benny kept his nose to the grindstone. He was enjoying sobriety, and he joined a health club and signed up with a personal trainer. A trip to the barber had trimmed his head and his beard.

One Saturday, he went looking for a tennis court to whack some balls. When he got to a playground in Somerville, Benny discovered the tennis courts were overrun by pickleball games. He put his racket and his canister of balls back into his car. Leaning on a fence, he watched a bevy of adults smacking a Whiffle ball across the net.

When one game finished, an older woman with a tan and wrinkles approached him.

"You've never played?" she asked.

"Never. I've heard about it."

"You're a tennis player."

"Yes, it's been a while. This looks interesting."

"It's addictive. Most of these players played tennis when they were younger. Pickleball puts less stress on tired joints and bones."

Benny grinned.

"If you're interested, there's an app to sign up for the calendar. The password is the city zip code."

"I just might. Thank you."

She stepped away; Benny got into his car.

Things are looking up. I've got Mrs. Fairchild in my corner. I'm feeling better.

Meanwhile to the north, Emma Wollensky sipped iced tea overlooking the Marginal Way at Clare Fairchild's summer retreat.

"Thanks for inviting me, Mrs. Fairchild."

"Emma, call me Clare."

"I've never been to Ogunquit. The traffic was crazy."

"It's the height of the summer."

"Your place, the view, the beach are all breathtaking."

"It's my happy place."

Emma shifted in her lawn chair. She hadn't thought to bring sunscreen and hoped she wouldn't roast. Her parents never had the time to go the beach. She wondered how much the value of the property was.

There has to be a reason for this visit, thought Emma. I'm not here just for iced tea.

Mrs. Fairchild took off her sunglasses. "Emma, do you think you have future at the museum?"

"I love my job."

"Good answer. But what's your dream job?"

"To be honest, Mrs. Fairchild, I mean Clare, I think it's coaching. My parents are jewelers; my brothers are financiers. I think my folks were surprised by my love of history and sports."

"Did your brothers play sports?"

"They did. They were good athletes, but they gave up sports to pursue their studies in college."

"And you played varsity hockey at school."

"It's what I lived for. I still play pickup."

"Good for you."

Why beat around the bush? "Why did you invite me here?"

"I wanted to talk to you off-campus, away from inquiring minds. I hope you'd stay with us, but you may leave us for your passion. I had a son, and his passion was hockey. So, I get it. If you stay with us, I can see you as the head of the operations."

"But Benny's here."

"He doesn't have tenure."

"You're going to fire him?"

"I didn't say that. He's on a short leash. This is just between us girls. Got it?"

"Yes."

Mrs. Fairchild sipped her drink.

"May I ask you a personal question?" asked the trustee.

"Sure." Emma wasn't sure where this was going, but she had a feeling, a very bad feeling.

"Do you have anyone in your life?"

"No."

"You're a very attractive young woman. I was curious."

"Why I don't have a man in my life?"

"I guess so."

"I never really have had one. I've dated, but there have been no long-term relationships. I don't lean that way."

"Your parents don't know."

"I've never said anything. I think my brothers know."

"You don't want your parents to be disappointed."

"They're very traditional."

"If they love you, they'll accept what you tell them."

"I pray to God for that."

"Thank you for sharing."

"You're the first."

"And not the last." They laughed. "How about some lunch? We'll get you out of the sun before you burn."

Forty

Wooden Ship Tour

Lizzie Soares checked into work. She waited out in the hall for Abbie to show up. Five minutes later, Abbie and her mother walked down the hall of the State House third floor. Lizzie waved to Claudia, who smiled at her on her way to the library.

"Your mother is a beauty," said Lizzie.

"I know. I can't compete with her," replied Abbie. "With her darker complexion rather than pale me, she looks like she could be your mother, not mine. Something wrong?"

"What're you doing for lunch?"

"Victor and I probably are going to eat on the Common."

"How about a trip to the *Constitution*?"

Abbie laughed. "Lizzie, you're feeling historical today, or do you want to see a certain guy interning near there?"

"Both. I haven't stepped on the ship for years, and I haven't seen that guy since last year."

"Do we have enough time?"

"If we hustle."

"That's a good hike. We'd get there and have to turn around."

"I'm okay with that."

Their overall boss, Mark Preston, had walked up behind them and overheard their conversation.

"You ladies want to visit the Charlestown Navy Yard at lunch?" he asked with a smile.

The teens were surprised by his appearance. Abbie said, "Mark, we didn't think we'd have enough time."

Preston pursed his lips. "I'm taking a half day to play in a charity golf tournament north of Boston this afternoon. I can drop you two off. How about that?"

Abbie said, "That would be great. Can I invite my friend from the library?"

"Sure. I have plenty of room. I'll tell Doc Ott you may be late coming back from lunch. I think it's great you want to visit one of our great historical sites."

Abbie stifled a chuckle.

Preston stepped into his office. Lizzie said, "I guess that settles that."

Abbie later called Victor about going. He was baffled by the plan. "You want to go to some old ship at lunch? What's the big deal?"

"History, Victor. *Old Ironsides* is the oldest ship in the Navy."

"I've never been there."

"C'mon, you might like it. It's not a swan boat."

"Okay." A thought came to him. "Hey, doesn't your ex-boyfriend work there?"

"Yes, my ex-boyfriend works there. Lizzie's the one who wants to see him."

"This seems a little odd. Maybe you should go without me."

"C'mon, Mark Preston's going to drop us off."

Victor loved being with Abbie, and Lizzie was very hot. In the car, he would suffer between two beauties.

"I'm in."

"See you at noon."

~ * ~

Gordon was still worried about his grandmother and his mother. He felt helpless about both of them. He wasn't used to sadness as a constant presence in his life. His father had no living relatives.

Summer noticed his demeanor. She tried to engage him in conversation a few times but was unsuccessful.

"Jack Quincy texted me and said he was going to grab me a sub and come over to eat lunch here at the yard."

Gordon nodded. "He said something like that to me on the way to work."

"Did you want to order a sub?"

"Nah, I brought my lunch."

"You'll hang with us?"

"I might find a spot to read."

"Oh, Mr. Anti-Social."

"Summer, Jack, and I take the train every day. It's not like I don't see him."

"We have fun when the three of us get together."

"I know. I just want to read. Jack will be more than happy to spend time with you."

"Okay, have it your way. You humbug."

"Just call me Ebenezer."

On the ride to Charlestown, Victor felt funny. He had sat in the back seat with Lizzie, which he didn't mind. Abbie had introduced Victor to their driver. Mark looked into the rearview mirror and saw Victor. The man stared; Victor stared. They held the glance for a moment. The teen was dazed. Mark Preston was startled for a moment.

Victor thought, *I've seen this guy around the building, but I hadn't looked into his eyes. That was weird.*

"It's nice to meet you, Victor." Mark smiled.

Just before noon, Gordon was taking out trash when a black Lincoln Navigator pulled near the entrance to the Navy Yard.

Who could this be? Vehicles usually don't get this close.

Out from the SUV emerged Abbie, Lizzie, and a guy. The girls saw Gordon and waved.

He was taken aback.

Who's the guy? Abbie's new boyfriend?

Gordon put down the trash barrel and walked over. The car driver rolled down his window.

"Hello, Gordon," he said.

"Oh, hi, Mr. Preston," replied Gordon.

"How's the job?"

"Great."

"I'm the chauffeur for these three folks. It's good to see you, Gordon."

"Same here, Mr. Preston. Please tell Doc Ott I said hi."

"Will do."

Preston waved and pulled away. On his ride, he drove in silence.

What was with that kid? Do I know him? Or do I feel I should know him.

Gordon looked at the three visitors. He knew the girls, not the guy.

"What're you doing here?" he asked. He hugged Lizzie.

Lizzie pointed to *Old Ironsides*. "We wanted a tour of the *Constitution*."

He laughed. "You, too, Abbie."

"Yes. This is Victor." Gordon shook his hand. It felt weird to shake with his successor. Victor was an inch shorter than him.

"Nice to meet you."

Victor felt awkward and figured he should've turned down this trip. "Same here."

Lizzie noticed two other teens approach.

Gordon introduced them to Summer and Jack. Abbie and Lizzie checked out their successor. It still felt weird to them.

Gordon put up a hand and said, "Let me empty the trash, and we can get in line."

They walked quickly to the ship. Who stood at the top of the gangplank but Mitch Ledowski.

"Mitch, are you switching ships?" asked Gordon.

"No, but I help out occasionally here. Who are your friends?" Gordon introduced all of them to Mitch.

"Welcome to the oldest ship in the U.S. Navy," he said. "She is undefeated in battle."

The six youths hovered around Mitch. "She was built across the water in the North End," he said, pointing. "She was launched in 1797 and cost $302,718.84. Some of her original cannons were borrowed from Castle Island."

Mitch started to pace in front of them. "The *Constitution* first spent time overseas in the war against the Barbary Pirates, but she gained her glory during the War of 1812. Her first, and most famous, sea battle occurred early in the war off New Jersey against the *H.M.S. Guerriere*. When a cannon shot failed to dent the *Constitution*, someone yelled. 'Her sides must be made of iron!' Thus, she became '*Old Ironsides*' forevermore.

"Her next two victories were fought against the *H.M.S. Java* off Brazil in December 1812, and she later battled off the coast of Africa against two smaller British ships, the *Cyane,* and the *Levant*. This battle, like the Battle of New Orleans, was fought after the war ended with the Treaty of Ghent."

"No internet then," said Jack.

"That's right, young man. Communication was very slow."

Mitch walked and pointed to a cannon. "The *Constitution* possessed a roster of four-hundred sailors, and she was designed as a forty-four-gun frigate, yet she carried fifty-four. There are twenty-four thirty-two-pound carronades, which this gun is. Below she carried thirty twenty-four-pounders and one eighteen-pound chase gun."

"Excuse me, sir," said Victor, "that gun next to you must weigh more than thirty-two pounds."

Mitch smiled. "You are correct. The weight refers to the shot itself. The heavier the shot, the more powerful it was. The lighter round had a longer range, but the carronades packed a powerful punch at a shorter distance."

His enthusiasm won over Jack and Victor. Several Navy sailors were decked out in historical garb. Gordon and Victor shot pictures with their phones.

Mitch waved at all the rigging. "Since this is a sailing vessel, she depends on the wind. There are thirty-seven sails totaling 42,720 feet of canvas. So, movement by water required many hands to deal with the sails. Look at these three masts. Imagine having to climb them."

"Now we'll go below," said the guide, and the six followed him.

Jack had to lean over to Gordon. "What were these people? Midgets?"

Mitch chuckled. "There weren't too many six-footers back then."

Their guide was about to continue his presentation when his phone rang. He looked at the number.

"Excuse me, it's my daughter." He cupped a hand to his left ear and stepped away.

Lizzie said, "He's got a lot of energy."

Victor walked around this level and shot more pictures. He wanted to draw a picture of this ship and maybe use it in a comic book.

"Mitch is a good guy," said Gordon. "He once served on the *Cassin Young* and taught history in high school."

Jack smirked. "No wonder you two get along."

Gordon walked toward a twenty-four-pound cannon and leaned on it. There was a flash of light enveloping the six teens. Several coughed. It settled.

He asked, "Did anyone see that?"

"See what, Gordon?" replied Lizzie. "Like the sun bursting from the sky?"

"Forget it." He looked around for Mitch. Maybe he had walked to the main deck.

Summer felt a little funny. "It was sunny a minute ago. Now it's cloudy. That's weird."

Abbie noticed it, too. "Gordon?"

The five looked at Gordon. Jack chipped in. "Gordon, has something funny happened? Why were we wrapped up in a cloud of light?"

Jack and Abbie knew of Gordon's tunnel history. Lizzie knew Gordon possessed a peculiar power, but she had never experienced it. Summer and Victor knew nothing of Gordon's forays into history.

Gordon flew topside. There were several sailors on board, not dressed in old uniforms. Next to the ship there was a long line of visitors. He stared at them. There was something peculiar about their apparel. Men wore hats, white shirts, and ties. Women sported dresses and kerchiefs. This wasn't 21st-century Boston.

Over at the dry dock, there was no DD 793. None of the many ships in the yard and the harbor were masted. There was no sign for the *Constitution* Museum. Looking to his right, he noted that the Boston skyline had shrunk. Only the Customs House towered above Boston.

That can't be. That's the old Boston Garden and a hotel next to it. Holy crap. What year is this?

Gordon grabbed a sailor.

"What is today's date?"

The sailor didn't look much older than Gordon. His name stenciled on his shirt read, "Conrad."

"June fourteenth, sir."

"Year?"

"I beg your pardon?" The sailor didn't have a Boston accent. Gordon couldn't tell where he was from.

"What year is it?"

He chuckled. "The same as yesterday. It's Sunday, June 14, 1931. The public's allowed to visit her before she's recommissioned."

"Thank you, Seaman Conrad."

"Hey, how did you get on board? The tour hasn't started."

Gordon flew down below.

1931? How did that happen? Wait. I touched that cannon. What is the key to getting back? Will these guys be freaked out below about being transported into 1931 during the Great Depression? Should I keep them here before I figure out what's going on?

When he returned to the group, Gordon could tell the gang was startled.

"Gordon, what's happening?" asked Abbie.

He looked at all of them. "I hate to tell you, but it's June, 1931. There's large group of tourists waiting to step on the ship, and there's a sailor chasing me."

At that moment, Seaman Conrad stood by them. "I'm sorry. I don't know how you folks got on board, but you must get back into line. The tour isn't starting for ten minutes. Please accompany me topside."

Gordon nodded, and they followed the sailor up the stairs to the main deck. When they got there, the six swiveled to check out the scene.

Yes, they stood on *Old Ironsides*, but like Gordon noticed, the immediate area had changed.

"Gordon," said Lizzie. "This can't be. Look at those people."

Jack said, "Oh, yes, it can. I've been with this guy before. It's happening."

Summer was perplexed. She whispered, "We're in a time warp."

Abbie said, "This is Gordon's specialty, literally jumping into the past."

"This can't be," said Summer, whose cheeks flushed with worry. "Boston's all different. Look at those people. They're wearing old clothes and old hairstyles. You're sure this isn't a reenactment?"

"No, it's not," Abbie responded.

Gordon said, "Let's step away from the ship before the sailor gives us any trouble."

Summer was nervous. She leaned on Gordon. "This isn't normal. Will we get back, Gordon?"

"I'm trying."

Abbie said, "He'll get us back."

Victor kept looking around at the Boston skyline. He recognized the white spire of the Old North Church. He wasn't sure how to react to the change in the scenery and the Boston skyline.

"This is weird," said Summer, who started to chew a fingernail.

Slowly, the group stepped down the gangplank amidst stares from the people who had lined up well in advance of visiting hours. Several adults cast looks of concern at these futuristic teens.

A little girl turned to her mother. "Mommy, those kids are wearing strange clothes."

"Quiet, dear," replied her mother. "Maybe their families don't have a lot of money for clothes."

Of the six, only Summer was visibly worried. Lizzie marveled at the transformation.

"Gordon, you did something like this last summer at the State House? Right?"

Gordon nodded. He was trying to come up with a password to the present.

Finally, they cleared the line of the tourists and walked in front of where the *Constitution* Museum would reside decades later.

They hovered around Gordon, their key to the future. Victor thought he was living in a movie. He tried to take pictures, but his phone had no power.

Abbie said, "Did you come up with anything?"

Gordon scratched his forehead. "*Old Ironsides!*" Nothing. "*Constitution!*" Nothing.

Summer grew more uncomfortable. "I'm stuck in 1931. My parents haven't even been born. What will I do here?"

"Summer, take a breath," said Jack, who hugged her. "I have faith in this guy."

Gordon paused. "I hope so, Jack. What else can I come up with? Did I touch anything?"

Lizzie slapped her thigh. "You touched the cannon before we were transported."

Gordon smiled. "*Guerriere!*"

Swoosh, a cloud of white light, and they returned to the right time. Their balance was unsteady for a moment, but it righted. They stood unexpectedly next to the *Constitution*. A different crowd lined up to board her.

Jack said, "Ladies and gentlemen, I think that concludes our tour of *Old Ironsides.*"

Victor said, "We've got to get back to work."

They started to walk toward the entrance of the park. A silver Mercedes SUV stopped and rolled down its window.

"Hello, Gordon," hailed Mrs. Fairchild. "Having a party?"

"A few friends came down on their lunch hour from their jobs at the State House. I gave them a quick tour of the *Constitution.*"

She said, "I'd be happy to give the State House folks a lift instead of walking. It's warm out."

The three nodded, and Victor, Abbie, and Lizzie hopped in.

Jack made his way back to work while Gordon and Summer walked back to the museum.

"I don't think I was ever so scared in my life, Gordon," said Summer. "Were you?"

"I was a little, but I had a feeling we'd get back."

Jack smiled. "You are one scary dude. No one would believe what happened today."

"So, keep it to yourself."

Summer kissed him on the cheek. "Thanks for getting us back." Then she hugged Jack.

Gordon exhaled. *Why does this happen? I love history, but it seems to find me at the oddest times and in the oddest places. How am I able to travel back in time? I'm no one special. I'm just a kid. Is this a gift, or is it a curse?*

Forty-one

You Have Another Child

Jack Fortune was tired, but it was a good tired. Readjusting to an infant brought back the drag of sleep deprivation. He and Theresa agreed he would take care of little Manny until midnight when she would relieve him. Jack couldn't believe he had a son. Granted, he had been named after Theresa's dad. What a delight the little guy was. Unlike with his first child, Abbie, Jack plunged into all the dirty tasks of bringing up a baby. Changing diapers and bathing didn't faze him.

The only downside of the new addition was that it cut into Jack's exercise, so he got up a little earlier. He either jumped on his Peleton bike for a quick ride or went to the health club before work.

The other downside was the loss of time with his daughter. He was so wrapped up with Manny he forgot about Abbie.

His ex-wife Claudia called him at work. "How's the baby?"

"He's great, Claudia."

"How's he sleeping?"

"Not too bad. He gets up just once a night."

"Abbie woke up several times before she settled down, but you wouldn't have noticed it, snoring away."

"Ouch, *mea culpa*. I'm better with this one."

Claudia smirked at her end of the phone. "I want you to do me a favor."

"Is your car giving you trouble?"

"I hardly use it. I commute to work."

"Oh, yeah. I forgot. What do you need?"

"Pay a little attention to Abbie. Facetiming and phone conversations aren't enough. I know you're busy, but she still needs you. You're very important to her."

"She's very important to me. How's her job?"

"We commute to Boston together. Two of her friends from school take the train as well, so they sit together and gab."

"How's Mark?" he asked. Even though Jack loved wife number two, he still carried feelings for wife number one. He was just a little jealous of her dating status. He knew Claudia had remained faithful during his five years away from home.

"He's good."

"Wedding bells in the future?"

"I don't think so. He's a lifelong bachelor, and I'm enjoying my freedom. One marriage was traumatic enough."

"Got it."

"See more of your daughter." She hung up.

The phone call dissolved Jack's good mood. He hadn't intentionally ignored Abbie. He had forgotten to squeeze her in.

Theresa was still on maternity leave and was itching to get back to the dealership, though she was surprised how much she loved being a mother.

Jack kissed her and the baby when he got home.

"What's up?" she asked, clearing the table. "You've hardly said a word. You told me nothing about your day."

"Claudia called."

She started to clear off the plates before putting them in the dishwasher. "Is she getting married?"

"No, nothing like that."

"She need a new car?"

"No."

"She want alimony?"

"No." Claudia had never asked him for alimony.

Theresa was getting agitated. "What the hell was she calling you for?"

"I haven't seen much of Abbie."

Theresa smiled. "I'm on Claudia's side on this."

"You are? How come?"

"She's your daughter. She still needs her dad. I lost mine when I was twelve. I missed him; I miss him now."

She went over to Jack and put her arm around him. "Jack, I appreciate what you've done with Manny. You're a great dad. You still have to be a great dad to Abbie. I know she thinks I'm a witch for marrying you."

"She doesn't think that."

"Really? You can't feel the ice in her eyes when she sees me."

"Really? I don't see that."

"Well, Jack Fortune, get off your ass and make arrangements to see Abbie. Manny and I can survive here."

"I do love you, Theresa."

"I love you, too. So does Abbie."

Forty-two

Mitch Is Confounded

With his new campaign to improve his health and physical well-being, Benny Goodman, during breaks and lunch, started to tour the Charlestown Navy Yard and the neighborhood. He made it to the top of the Bunker Hill Monument, enjoyed the view, and walked back to work. His diet steered him away from takeout and sweets. He enjoyed cooking new meals. Benny prayed the pounds would start to melt away. He felt better.

Benny sauntered over to the *Cassin Young*. He enjoyed Mitch Ledowski's attitude.

I hope I'm as chipper as Mitch if I get to eighty.

Mitch stood in front of the destroyer's entrance. Benny called him, but Mitch failed to respond with his usual gusto.

"Mitch?" Benny stood next to him.

Mitch was roused from his distraction.

"You okay?"

"That Gordon. There's something about him. I can't explain it."

"How do you mean?"

"I told you how I thought he disappeared on this ship. Yesterday, I was over at the *Constitution* giving tours when he showed up with the other intern and four other kids."

"It was lunch, right? What was wrong?"

"I started the tour. They were enthusiastic. Gordon and this other kid shot pictures. When I took them below, I stepped away because my daughter called. My granddaughter's leg was being operated on, so I took the call. I walked away from them. After I talked to my daughter, they had disappeared."

"Did they go below?"

"I asked a couple of the sailors. They didn't see anybody below decks."

"So, what else happened?"

"I returned to the entrance to start another tour. They reemerged a short time later near the ship's entrance. The intern Summer was pale and shaking like she had seen a ghost."

"Was there anything else unusual about their reappearance?"

"I don't think so. I can't explain it, but they looked relieved. I just found the whole incident strange. Maybe it's just my doddering mind playing tricks on me."

"Thanks, Mitch. I'll see what I can find out."

When Benny got back to the museum, he saw Clare Fairchild talking to Gordon. As he got closer, he overheard them.

"Thank you for giving my friends a ride back to work, Mrs. Fairchild," said Gordon with a broom in his hand.

"Gordon," she said, "it was my pleasure. By the way, those two young ladies are former girlfriends." He blushed. "Now, Summer's your friend. You do get around."

"Not really," answered Gordon.

Mrs. Fairchild saw Benny and waved. Gordon swept up broken glass a customer had left in the entrance hall.

"Hello, Ben."

He nodded.

"Mrs. Fairchild, may I borrow Mr. Beckwith for a moment?"

"Certainly, you have a good day. We'll talk soon about the fall exhibit."

Gordon emptied the rest of the debris into a barrel.

Benny curled his right forefinger at Gordon, who put down his broom.

The two walked around the corner of the museum toward the Marines Quarter building.

Benny halted and turned to Gordon. "What am I going to do with you, Gordon?"

Gordon was surprised. "What? Did I do something wrong?"

His boss said, "The summer's almost over, thank God. What's up with you? Mitch is concerned you are some sort of sorcerer. He thinks you have a habit of disappearing from the yard's two-star attractions. You also have a chummy relationship with the chairwoman of the board of trustees. How did you manage that? I'm the director, and I don't have that kind of relationship with her. It's too late in the season to fire you. But I have an idea I want to test out. Tomorrow, you and I will take a tour of the *Cassin Young*."

As they walked back to the museum, Gordon wasn't sure how to respond to this. Benny Goodman hadn't been very friendly to him all summer. He liked Emma Wollensky better.

Do I admit to this guy what happened? What if I take him on the ship and we're transported?

It bothered him all day, and on the way home. Jack and Abbie kept up their own conversation while he pretended to read.

He also was waiting to hear the latest news about his grandmother.

Forty-three

The Tin Can

The morning soured quickly for Gordon. First, his mother said, "Grandma is doing poorly. They're putting her into hospice."

"That's where terminally ill people go," chimed in his father.

"I know, Dad," snapped Gordon.

"I'm driving up this morning," his mother added. "Dad will take you after work."

"I'll call in sick."

Marty put his hand up. "No, Gordon, don't call in sick if you're not. It's a bad habit to start. I've had several knuckleheads who work for me pull that a lot."

Gordon laughed. "And they don't work for you anymore."

Martha rubbed her son's back. "Dad's right. I'll see you later."

Gordon's eyes started to water. "Will she die before Dad and I get there?"

"Grandma's bad, but they expect her to hang on for a while. Otherwise, I'd tell you to come with me."

Marty smiled. "Don't worry, Gordon. Your grandmother is a tough old bird."

"Okay."

Gordon said very little to his friends enroute to work. He and Jack stepped off the subway in the North End.

"What's up, Gordon?" asked Jack.

"It's my grandmother, my mother's mother, is dying."

"That sucks. Are you close?"

"I didn't get to know her until recently. For years, she didn't approve of my dad as the husband of her youngest daughter."

"What's wrong with your dad?"

"Nothing, but my grandmother wanted Mom's high school sweetheart to be her husband. Jack, get this... this guy, Curtis Bakewell, is now the mayor of the city they grew up in. I've met him, and I can tell he still likes my mother."

"Awkward!" Jack howled.

"Really crazy. I'm going up to Maine after work today with my father."

They reached the gates of the park. "Good luck with your grandma."

"Thanks, Jack."

Gordon checked in with Emma, who told him to stand by. Summer reported a few minutes later. Usually, Emma gave out assignments to the interns first thing in the morning.

"Gordon, what's up?" asked Summer.

"Emma told me to wait. I have a feeling Benny's after me."

Summer grinned. "Does he know about your special talent?"

"He suspects. I think Mitch might have said something about our tour of the *Constitution*. I also think he's pissed because Mrs. Fairchild is friendly to us and not to him."

"We just ran into her in Ogunquit."

"I know that."

"What's Benny going to do? Fire you with a week left on the job?"

"I hope not."

"You haven't done anything bad. You're a good worker. Emma likes you."

Benny Goodman stepped into the office. He pointed and curled his right index finger at him. "Gordon, come with me. Leave your backpack."

"Where are we going?"

"For a little walk."

As they were leaving, Gordon turned to Summer and raised his hands in prayer. Summer suppressed a laugh.

The director and the intern exited the museum and headed for DD 793, a.k.a. the *U.S.S. Cassin Young*. There was no Mitch Ledowski when they arrived at the entrance.

Gordon was surprised by his absence. "Where's Mitch?"

Benny snapped, "He had a family issue. He won't be in today."

They stepped onto the ship. Even anchored, Gordon felt as if the ship were sailing on the ocean.

Benny started to pace on the main deck. "What's your secret?"

"What?"

"How do you disappear?"

"What?"

"Don't bullshit me, Gordon Beckwith. There's something different about you. Mitch thinks you have a special ability to disappear on this ship and on *Old Ironsides*. If so, I want you to transport me. I need material for my history of the Navy Yard and a fall exhibition about any ghosts."

"I have no special talent. For some unknown reason, I feel like I have a connection with history. It's only happened a few times."

"Where have you gone and who have you met?"

"To colonial America. I've met George Washington and Benedict Arnold."

"Together?"

"Separately."

Benny frowned. "You're putting me on."

Maybe this is a big waste of time, thought Benny. *Maybe Mitch imagined this. Maybe this kid is full of crap.*

Benny stood next to Gordon. "Mitch is wrong. You're just busting my balls. George Washington and Benedict Arnold. Ha! Bullshit!"

"You asked."

Gordon was incensed this guy was giving him a hard time. He didn't fault Benny for doubting him. Now his boss was calling him a liar. He headed for midship and opened a door. Benny followed him inside. Gordon touched the portrait of Cassin Young, and everything changed.

The sea rocked below, and Gordon felt nauseous. The ship crested a wave. Benny also became queasy. A sailor came up to the two of them.

"What are you two civvies doing here without a helmet and a life jacket?" he asked.

The two didn't know what to say.

"If you're on the main deck, helmet and life preserver are required." The sailor looked at them. "Where did we pick you two up? Okinawa?"

Gordon nodded.

"What papers do you work for? I'm from Illinois outside of the Chicago. Do you have cameras?"

Gordon wasn't sure how to respond. Benny Goodman was good for nothing. He was paralyzed with fear.

The sailor stared at Gordon. "You're awfully young looking. Did you get a deferment from serving?"

"I, I look younger than I am. I have a heart murmur."

The sailor laughed. "A tin can, the *U.S.S. Cassin Young* in the Pacific Ocean is no place for a guy with a heart murmur. We're on picket duty here off Okinawa trying to protect the bigger ships from kamikazes."

Benny knew Gordon wasn't lying, and he wondered what the date was. His mouth finally relaxed. When he heard the sailor mention Okinawa, Benny knew it was definitely 1945. The bloody campaign had lasted from April 1, 1945 to June 22, 1945.

Gordon queried, "What's today's date? I'm all goofed up after we passed the International Dateline."

The sailor said, "I believe it's July 30 in the good year of our Lord 1945."

Benny and Gordon knew of the date's significance in the destroyer's history, the last kamikaze attack of the war. The *Cassin Young* had experience with the suicidal planes trying to damage U.S. ships—she had been hit by one in April.

The sailor left and returned with two helmets and two life preservers. "Put these on."

Both visitors pulled on the preservers and helmets. "What papers you work for?"

Gordon snapped, "*Bangor Daily News.*"

Benny said, "*Lynn Daily Item.*"

The sailor said, "I've got a buddy from Maine. I'll go see if he's off duty."

Gordon had a feeling who that buddy was.

Benny said, "Gordon, how the hell do we get back?"

"Usually, I need a word."

"Great, you need a word. The English language is vast."

"Not that drastic, it's something that usually connects to the time or the place."

"You had better hurry up. I don't want to be killed in 1945."

"Neither do I."

Ten minutes later, the sailor brought back his buddy. "This here is Seaman Buster McKinley, the pride of Bath, Maine."

Buster wasn't as fresh-faced as when Gordon had met him at Pearl Harbor. His face was leaner, but he was imposing at six-feet two and two hundred pounds. The interlopers introduced themselves.

"Gordon, you look familiar," said Seaman McKinley. "Have we met?"

"Not really."

"I usually don't forget a face. How are things in Maine?"

"I've been gone for a while."

"Four years for me. I left before I graduated high school." McKinley kept staring at Gordon. "What I really miss is hockey. Can't play out here. I haven't skated in ages. Do you play?"

"A little."

"You're too thin for a defenseman and too small for a goalie. Forward?"

"Yes."

"Are you fast?"

"Pretty fast."

"I gotta get back to my duties. It was nice to meet you two."

Buster and his shipmate took off. Gordon didn't tell Benny of his connection to Seaman McKinley.

Benny said, "Let's go outside."

When they stepped out into the darkness, there were men at their stations. Gordon wondered how many guys out of the three hundred were on duty. Where was his grandfather stationed on the destroyer?

Benny tamped down his stomach. He had stepped back into the late days of World War II. Germany already had surrendered; Japan hung on. Two atomic bombs would be released in the next month ending the world's deadliest war.

How could he use this ability of Gordon's? Could he go back with Gordon to a specific era in history? Holy crap! As a historian, this would be a gateway to be an eyewitness to history. It would be great for his history of the Navy Yard. He could write other books and make his reputation as a world-class historian. Benny

Goodman wouldn't have to dig in libraries and archives ...he would take a first-class seat to history.

The two stood on the port side of the ship. Benny got the urge for discovery and headed for the starboard side of the ship.

Gordon had a bad feeling. "Benny, don't go over there!"

"What?" he replied. Benny couldn't make out Gordon's voice with the rollicking of the waves.

Gordon fought the urge to puke. Just as Benny disappeared, guns started to fire at an incoming aircraft. The noise hurt their ears.

Kamikaze? Gordon asked himself. *What side of the ship was it supposed to hit?*

The biplane with its attached bomb crashed into the starboard side of the main deck. The explosion shredded some sailors and knocked others off their feet. The firing ceased.

Gordon ran over to the other side. One sailor was attached to the 40-millimeter gun and looked okay except for the lifeless eyes. Another sailor was stretched out on the deck missing his head. Blood and body parts were strewn about. Gordon vomited over the side.

Where was Benny Goodman?

A bunch of sailors worked on putting out a fire caused by the crash. Gordon couldn't find his boss.

Seaman McKinley found Gordon. "Hey, I know you're a civvie, but could you help us move some ammo away from the five-inch gun? We don't want another boom."

"Sure," replied Gordon.

With other members of the crew, Gordon lifted heavy shells from a storage area away from this gun to a safer side of the deck. Working at his father's businesses and weightlifting for hockey made the job easier. The heat from the flames and the tropical humidity proved to be trying. He gasped for air. Sweat dripped from every pore.

Gordon crouched. Buster McKinley stopped and held out a cup of water. "Thanks for your help. I found your buddy. He's inside the wardroom."

Gordon gulped down the warm water. It wasn't a cold bottle of Poland Springs, but he didn't care. "Is he okay?"

"I think he's a little dazed from the excitement. Otherwise, he's fine."

"Great."

"You two will have plenty to write, if the censors let you."

Gordon handed the cup back to Buster who was about to step away. "Hey, wait. I knew you looked familiar."

"Do I?" Gordon couldn't believe this sailor would be his grandfather.

Buster slapped his forehead. "Pearl Harbor! You were on the *Vestal*. Weren't you?"

Gordon wasn't sure if he should lie. He whispered, "Yes."

"Why aren't you in uniform? Were you invalidated out of the service? How did you become a reporter?"

Gordon just looked at him. His mouth was immobilized; he couldn't respond.

"There's something funny about you. I feel I should know you from home. Are you from Maine?"

"Boston, but my mother's from Maine."

"Where in Maine?"

"Bath."

Buster punched him lightly on the shoulder. "No way! I'm from Bath. I'll probably know her family. What's her name?"

"Martha, Martha Beckwith." Gordon didn't offer her maiden name to her father.

"I don't know any Beckwiths in Bath." Buster took off his cap and scratched his head.

"It was good to see you again." Buster walked about twenty feet when he turned and hurled another question. "Was that her maiden name?"

Gordon pretended not to hear on his way to the wardroom. He waved his hands in the air.

He found Benny without his helmet and a small gash over his right eye.

"You okay, Benny?" Gordon asked.

"I can't believe I survived the blast. You knew the kamikaze was going to happen because you had read up on the ship's history. Right?"

"Yes, I tried to get you to stop, but you didn't hear me."

"I can't believe the carnage I saw. The destruction to the ship with the gore splattered around the deck was horrible. These Navy guys are incredible."

"They are." He wanted to tell his boss about his grandfather, but he didn't.

"Can we get out of here? I'd like to go back to where we belong. I've had enough living history."

Benny would return to libraries and archives searching for historical information.

"I think so."

Gordon stepped outside. He yelled, "Kamikaze!"

A flash of light. Another incoming kamikaze? No, the two travelers had returned to Charlestown at the stern entrance to DD793.

Benny still sported a bandage over his right eye. He felt it, it was real, and it hurt.

"Thanks for getting us home. I'm sorry for being such a dick about you. You are truly an unusual kid. I think I'd like to go home. I'm tired and sore. See you on Monday."

Gordon felt the same way. On the way home, he collapsed on the train. Jack Quincy had to rouse him several times to get him out of the car when they reached Tiot.

When they got off the train, Jack looked at Gordon on the platform. "Don't tell me you went travelling again?"

"Yup."

"Want to talk about it? You reek of BO and salt water. Gordon, you need to shower. I don't think you went swimming."

"Not today, Jack. Maybe another time."

Forty-four

Final Departure

Marty picked up Gordon at home. Gordon had showered quickly, and he was still exhausted after the day's exploit. They battled rush hour traffic through Massachusetts, New Hampshire, and into Maine. Gordon snoozed through most of the trip. Marty left him alone. He figured his son was pooped from work. They made it to the McKinley household after nine o'clock. Martha greeted them at the door.

"How is she?" asked Marty.

"In and out. The doctor just left."

"What about your siblings?"

"They're still out of state. They'll probably get here too late."

Marty put his arm around his wife. "How are you?"

Martha's eyes were watery. "I'm okay, better with you two here."

Gordon had never seen his mother look this upset. She had always lived on the sunnier side of life, but her mother's illness had taken its toll on her.

Martha hugged Gordon. "She wants to see you, Gordon. Be yourself."

At that moment, the doorbell rang. Martha opened the door to Mayor Curtis Bakewell. "Hi, Martha."

She introduced Marty. They shook hands. The mayor wore another beautiful suit. Bakewell saw Gordon. "Hi, Gordon."

"Hi, Mr. Mayor."

Bakewell wasn't sure what to do next. "I heard Agnes wasn't feeling well."

She put her hand on Bakewell's back. "Curtis, this isn't a good time, but thanks for coming by."

Without protest, he left.

Marty laughed. "That was my competition. He's a pretty boy. Figures he ended up a politician."

"Marty, he's not a bad guy."

"But he still carries the torch for you."

Gordon cut in. "Yes, he does, Mom. Every time we've run into him, he lights up."

Martha blushed. "Enough, you two. Gordon, go see your grandmother."

Gordon walked upstairs to Agnes' bedroom. A fan blew lightly. He expected his grandmother to be at death's door. Instead, she was propped up against the headboard reading the newspaper. Her hair had been combed, and Martha had refreshed her mother's makeup.

"Hi, Gordon," she said. "Come up and sit next to me."

Gordon started to untie his sneakers. She waved him off. "Who cares if I die with dirty bed covers?"

"Grandma, are you going to be okay?"

"Gordon, I'm not, but I'm almost ninety. I've had a good life. I've been blessed. One of my few regrets is that I didn't get to know you better."

She took his right hand in her left. "Your father is a good man. I was too stubborn to accept him. Martha couldn't have done better. I like Curtis, but he blew his chance years ago."

"He just came by."

"That was nice of him, but he's not family. I had high hopes for Curtis, but the Ivy League and making money in New York took him away for too long. My other children live too far away to see me off."

She sighed. "Did you read Buster's letters?"

"Yes, thanks for giving them to me."

"I thought you would have liked to have known him as a younger person."

"He saw a lot of action."

"That he did."

Agnes slipped back onto her pillow. "I'm getting a little tired."

"Are you okay?"

"I'm with my grandson," answered Agnes, her voice fading. "I've really enjoyed our recent time together."

Gordon wasn't sure whether to call for his mother and father. Agnes still held his hand.

"Gordon, I wish you could've met Buster."

She closed her eyes. Gordon had a bad feeling, a feeling of helplessness.

"But I did, Grandma."

Agnes slowly opened her eyes.

"I know. Goodbye." And she closed her eyes and died.

Gordon released his hand from his grandmother's. Tears cascaded down his cheeks. His parents then appeared in the bedroom. Martha went over and hugged Gordon. They both cried quietly. Even Marty had shed a tear.

Gordon had never experienced such loss in his life. He hoped he would never ever have to feel that way again.

Epilogue

Agnes Swenson McKinley was buried beside her husband, Buster. The Beckwiths attended the funeral Mass with Martha's sisters and brothers who had arrived on Saturday. They departed two days later. Martha was named as her mother's executrix, and she stayed in Bath for a week, cleaning up her childhood home and getting it ready for sale. Her mother had left the estate in perfect order and had even picked out the readings and hymns for her funeral. None of her siblings wanted any part of Bath. Gordon had got to meet his McKinley aunts and uncles. Other than introductions, there was little or no conversation with them.

At home, Marty and Gordon fended for themselves. Marty spent most nights grilling in the back yard; the other nights they got takeout.

During Gordon's last week of work, Benny Goodman had taken personal time, so he didn't say goodbye to his interns or wish them well. The teens debated whether their boss was really ill.

Gordon and Summer ate a final lunch in the North End. Jack stayed away that day, leaving them alone. The two grabbed pizza and walked around the neighborhood. They stopped in the Paul Revere Mall.

Summer said, "It's been quite a summer. I meet a great guy, I take a trip into the past, and my parents are staying together. I probably will never see you again, and you'll probably hook up again with your old girlfriend. She may have a new boyfriend, but the fire still burns brightly for Gordon Beckwith."

"I doubt it, Summer."

She smiled. "Some guys just don't get it."

Gordon finished a cannoli from Bova Bakery. He wiped his mouth with a napkin.

"I wish you lived closer, Summer."

"Me too."

"We had a good time in Ogunquit."

"You have my number." She kissed him in front of a horde of tourists, who paid the two no attention. They walked back to the museum hand in hand.

"By the way, my parents are going to marriage counseling," she said. "Dad got a new job and promised not to cheat. Mom, too."

"That's a good thing."

"I hope so."

At the end of the workday, Emma Wollensky shook their hands and wished them well. "We hope you come back next summer."

Gordon shrugged.

Summer said, "Can I think on it? You'll be here, Emma."

"No, I won't be here."

"What do you mean, Emma?"

"I'm taking a job teaching phys ed and coaching the girls' hockey team at Dedham High School."

"You'll be great," said Gordon.

"It's something I've always wanted to do. I'm following my dream, much to my parents' disappointment."

Gordon grinned. "They'll get over it."

"I hope so."

At four o'clock, Summer jumped into her Jeep and waved goodbye to Gordon and Jack Quincy.

Not far away on Beacon Hill, Abbie Fortune and Victor Santos were saying their goodbyes.

"We can still see each other," she said.

"Abbie, I still think you like the freaky blond guy. He seems like a good guy, but he's different."

"We'll be getting our licenses this year."

"Abbie, I don't know."

"Victor, call me or text me. I like being with you. We could still go to the MFA. Hopefully, we'll have the same jobs next summer."

"Me too."

They kissed outside the library entrance.

Victor wasn't sad about the breakup. He told Gus Saunders about it on the way home.

"Hey, Victor, there are plenty of fish in the sea. That's why you take advantage of it when you're a single guy."

"I know, but I really liked her. She was a cool cat."

"You never know. You may run into her again in the future."

"I'd like that."

Victor unlocked his front door. He set the kitchen table for his mother, who would be late.

She showed up an hour later with food from a Brazilian restaurant. They ate quietly.

After they cleaned up the table, she said, "I've never told you about your father. I think it's time."

"I don't know if he's alive, dead, or in prison."

"Victor, you know I went to U-Mass Boston. It was all I could afford. A few years after I graduated, and I was working at the

Carney Hospital, I met this guy who was a little older than me. He had just started out in politics. He had been a lawyer, but he was ambitious. We started to go out. Later, I found out I was pregnant. And me, a nurse, not taking care of my birth control. I told him, and he told me to get an abortion. I refused, and he cut me off. I thought he loved me, but he loved himself."

"Have you seen him since?"

"No."

"Does he know who I am?"

"No."

"Who is he, Mom?"

She said, "Mark Preston."

"The secretary of state, a guy who gave me a ride the other day? Shit! He goes out with Abbie's mother, my boss."

"Wow. Now you know. I figured you're old enough to know and old enough to decide if you want to reach out to him."

"Did you love him?"

"I thought I did."

"But the asshole dumped you when you got pregnant with me."

"That's correct."

Victor started to pace the floor. He grew angry, knowing he's been deprived of a father and of knowing who his father was. Plenty of his buddies didn't have or know their fathers. Skinny's dad was serving time for armed robbery.

One of these days I'll confront Mr. Mark Preston, the son-of-a-bitch. Maybe, I'll punch him in the mouth for making my mother suffer, or maybe I'll ignore him like he's ignored us.

~ * ~

Victor's mood lifted a few days later when he received a small package.

His mother asked, "Who's it from?"

Victor couldn't wait to open it. He saw the return address. "It's from a friend."

"From the wrapping, I don't think it's from Skinny." Victoria suppressed a smile. Neighbor Gus had tipped her off.

Victor tore open the wrapping. It was a book on Isabella Stewart Gardner Museum. That made his week.

~ * ~

Mark Preston finally told Claudia about his past and asked her to marry him. She was disappointed.

"I'm sorry, Mark," she replied. "One marriage was trying enough. I'm not sure if you're totally trustworthy after what you just told me. I've enjoyed our time together, but you can get ready to announce your campaign for governor as a proud bachelor."

Mark wasn't surprised. Claudia was a woman of her convictions. He respected her. He just wasn't sure if he loved her.

~ * ~

Benny Goodman clicked the Send button on his email offering his resignation to Clare Fairchild. He thanked her for the opportunity to work at the museum, but it was time to devote to his writing and maybe some teaching. After a review of his research on the Navy Yard, Benny was ready to write the book he had put off for too long. He exhaled after sending the email, but he felt good.

Benny had visited his ex-wife Tovah at her Rockport studio. There was no animosity between the two of them. He had closure.

His experience with Gordon Beckwith had freaked him out.

Did that really happen? Was I really on the Cassin Young? *No one would believe me, but I'm going to pick up my life and move forward.*

He bought a pickleball paddle and joined a league.

Clare Fairchild later read the email with a grin. She was sad that Emma wouldn't be available to succeed Benny, but she was happy for both people following their own paths.

Now, she said, to herself, we have to fill two positions at the museum. Such is life.

~ * ~

Lizzie Soares loved sharing an adventure with Gordon, but she knew they had no future. Lizzie couldn't believe her trip into the past. She wasn't worried they'd get back. She knew Gordon would find a way. What they had the previous summer was nice, but the physical distance was too much. She liked Abbie Fortune. Besides, Lizzie was dedicated to wrapping up her senior year in the classroom and on the ice. She was hoping a hockey scholarship would help defray her college expenses. Her father had assured her that he and her mother would pay for college.

Gary said. "Undergrad we will cover. Postgrad may fall on you, but you never know."

~ * ~

Jack Quincy was fired up for football season. Working a full-time job was fine to build up his bank account, but his passion was playing on the beautiful artificial turf at Tiot High School. Although he hoped to receive a football scholarship, Jack still wanted to play college ball at a Division Two or Three school. He would concentrate on his marks.

His father Bradley asked him about his job. "Dad, I'll be honest. I was humping all summer. But you know what? I gained an appreciation of what you do. It's a tough job. You and your people do great work to help folks who are injured or hurt get back on their feet and feel better. I could see the difference with some of them."

"Thanks for that. Would you like to do that for a living?"

"I'm not sure. Maybe something in sports medicine."

"Northeastern University has a good program."

"Expensive place."

"If you get in, we'll try to work something out."

~ * ~

While Jack started double sessions for football, Abbie and Gordon practiced with their respective soccer teams. Abbie liked the fact the boys' and girls' teams worked out next to each other.

On the first day of practice, she started to walk home when a familiar face pulled up outside of school in his car.

Abbie saw him wave to her. "Dad?"

She ran over to him when he got out of his car and hugged him. He kissed her on the cheek. "Hi, honey."

"What're doing here?"

"Taking my favorite daughter out for driving lessons."

"I'm starving and hot. Can I go home first to shower?"

"Tell you what. We'll go out to eat before for any driving lesson."

"Sweet."

During their meal, Jack enjoyed Abbie telling him about her day and what happened during the summer. He could almost kick himself for not making himself more available to Abbie. She was a great kid.

~ * ~

Gordon Beckwith had seen very little of Moose Marini during the summer. Moose had started football alongside Jack Quincy. Finally, the two friends got together on Labor Day weekend before the start of the new school year. After three games of wiffleball, they biked over to Seven Eleven. Gordon bought a Gatorade while Moose picked up Twinkies, a Devil Dog, and a one-liter bottle of Mountain Dew.

"Moose, what're you doing?"

"Double sessions are dehydrating me. I need to bulk up."

"With nutrients, not sweets."

"It's my comfort food."

Gordon laughed. "Your line coach won't be handing you Devil Dogs at halftime when you're gassed from playing."

"It's a nice thought, Gordon, but it's not going to happen."

Gordon had brought Moose up to speed about all the events from the past several months.

"Jesus, Gordon, you got another babe? Jack Quincy told me all about her." Moose slurped soda and inhaled the last portion of his Devil Dog. "And you found more portals to the past."

"Yes, I thought I was done with that."

"As the man touched by history, I don't think you'll ever lose that power. Are you going back there next summer?"

"No, my dad got me a nice, safe job as a counselor at the YMCA in Foxborough, five minutes from his store. Maybe you and Jack can work there, too."

"Taking care of little kids?"

"I guess so. Playing games, teaching them sports."

Moose smiled. "So, no ships, no secret passages, and no tunnels."

Gordon smiled. "I'll be outdoors most of the time. I should have no worries. It should be a quiet summer."

Meet Mike Ryan

A Boston native, Mike Ryan has worked as a teacher, reporter, communications specialist, and freelance writer. He holds a bachelor's degree in history from Boston State College and a master's degree in journalism from Boston University. His byline has appeared in newspapers and magazines. He has written ten novels and suffers from a serious addiction to book stores. He lives with his family southwest of Fenway Park.

Other Works from the Pen of

Mike Ryan

George Washington Ate Here! *-* A teenager grabs a magic key to the library and recruits George Washington to prevent the decimation of the town's Fourth of July celebration.

Benedict Arnold Wasn't A Bum - Gordon Beckwith has a knack for dealing with magic tunnels. Last year he met George Washington; this year Gordon meets Benedict Arnold.

Dear reader,

I hope you've enjoyed reading this tale of a boy's unusual
gift.

Your opinion is valuable to other
readers like you,
who may be looking for books like mine.

Please consider taking a few minutes to post a review,
however brief,
on the site where you purchased this book
or on the Wings ePress web page.

You may also want to visit my author page
at the Wings' website, where you can find
all the other books in my series.

Thank you!

Mike Ryan

Visit Our Website

For The Full Inventory
Of Quality Books:

<u>Wings ePress, Inc</u>

Quality trade paperbacks and downloads
in multiple formats,
in genres ranging from light romantic comedy to general
fiction and horror.
Wings has something for every reader's taste.
Visit the website, then bookmark it.
We add new titles each month!

Wings ePress, Inc.
3000 N. Rock Road
Newton, KS 67114